Joseph Converse Heywood

Salome, a Dramatic Poem

Joseph Converse Heywood

Salome, a Dramatic Poem

ISBN/EAN: 9783744708234

Printed in Europe, USA, Canada, Australia, Japan

Cover: Foto ©Andreas Hilbeck / pixelio.de

More available books at **www.hansebooks.com**

SALOME.

A DRAMATIC POEM.

BY

J. C. HEYWOOD.

NEW YORK:

PUBLISHED BY HURD AND HOUGHTON,

459 BROOME STREET.

1867.

" I shall therefore speak my mind here at once briefly: That neither did any other city ever suffer such miseries, nor any age ever breed a generation more fruitful in wickedness than this was, from the beginning of the world."

FLAVIUS JOSEPHUS.

SALOME.

$\blacklozenge$

A Chamber in Jerusalem.

CHORUS OF CHRISTIANS.

CHORUS.

WHAT should it mean?
 The Dweller in the holy place,
The Cherubim between,
 Hath turned away His face.

  How long, O Lord, how long?
  Shall wrath abide forever?
And awful darkness of Thy frown,
To nether darkness pressing down,
  Be lifted never?
  O Lord, how long?

  How long, O Lord, how long?
  In mercy wield Thy power.
Oh save us with Thine outstretched hand,
Keep in its hollow still this band,

Through this dread hour.
O Lord, how long?

Enter SALOME *and* THONA.

SALOME.

Why tremble ye, my friends? What terrors
new
Have overcome your faith? He is with you
Who said, all-powerful still His to defend,
Lo! I am with you even to the end.

CHORUS.

What! heard ye not the tale?
    They whisper it with bated breath,
With staring eyes, and visage pale,
    As fearful men appointed unto death.

SALOME.

Dread harbingers descend, portents appear,
But fear not ye, our Guardian is near.

CHORUS.

They came, they came all solemnly and slow,
From trembling tombs,
In silent woe,
The shades of priests long dead,
And shuddering glooms

Of midnight grew more dark and dread.
With noiseless tread,
In semblances of priestly vestments clad,
With supplicating look,
Beseeching, outstretched hands that shook,
And faces pale and sad,
They took
The way unto the Temple's Eastern gate,
In show of consecrated state.
While on the hills around,
The tribes from opening graves,
From yawning burial caves,
Without or voice or sound,
Gathered themselves in hosts,
Gazing, pallid ghosts.
The Temple's Eastern gate,
Whose ponderous weight
The strength of twenty men can scarce unfold,
Untouched upon its hinges rolled.
And, through its port,
On, on into the inner court,
The dread procession went,
With heads low bent.
From every hill,
The gathered hosts
Of ghosts
Gazed still.
Then from the Holy Place

About the altar shone a light,
So bright
No mortal face
Could stand before it.
The hosts
Of gathered ghosts
Bow and adore it.
Then o'er the Temple came
Darkness, dread and black.
Around it myriad forms of flame
Moved with a fiery track.
To its unfolding bosom passed the Light,
And rose from sight
Into the heavens, which seemed to roll
In terror backwards on the pole.
And then was heard,
Like thunder roaring through the sky,
A deep and awful cry,
Speaking this word :
Come out from her, and be ye separate.
And, when this voice had cried,
Out-rolling from the Eastern gate
Another voice replied,
A cry, such as, till then, man never heard,
Speaking this word :
Let us go hence.
And thence
The phantom throng

Turned in flight headlong,
Rushing to their graves, therein to hide
From coming terrors they could not abide.

SALOME.

Thy keeper, Judah, hath abandoned thee,
And summoned all His faithful ones to flee.
Yet greater wrath is coming, and to-night
May overthrow this nation, in His sight
A barren tree encumbering the ground,
On which, these many years, naught good is
     found.
Accursed it falls, the solid earth upheaves
With its bent roots, and scatters poisonous leaves.

CHORUS.

Wail! Israel, wail!
Through all the scattered lands
Where now ye rove,
O'er burning sands,
In pestilential grove,
Or snowy regions pale.

Wail! Israel, wail!
Not for the unnumbered woes
Ye suffer there,
But for the woe that goes
Into the House of Prayer
Where prayers no more avail.

Wail! Israel, wail!
Not that your name is lost,
Not that, as broken pieces of a wreck are tossed,
The storms and billows drive you on their way
To where no day
Invites a venturous sail.

Wail! Israel, wail!
Not that the winds of heaven
Can find you not, nor yet the stars of even ;
But for Jerusalem bereft of God,
Her children perishing beneath the rod :
Wail! Israel, wail!

SALOME.

Yea, well may agonizing Israel say,
Alas! for woful Judah, cast away!
Lament ye, too, for us ; pray, lest we faint,
By miseries overcome, of doubts attaint.

CHORUS.

Lord, let us suffer still, if it may be
Our sufferings only drive us nearer Thee.
But if, too strong, they tempt us to complain,
Ease, pitying One, somewhat, the tempting pain.
So that in patience we may here abide,
Until the Bridegroom come to call His bride.

[*Exit* CHORUS.

THONA.

Fruitless again the search; nor food, nor wine,
Nor aught that healthful palates could endure.
And, led forth now by Want, all-conquering,
E'en from the inner chamber where he sat
In ghastly power, grim Famine stalks the streets
A skeleton, and holds the citadel.

SALOME.

Ah! poor Bernice!

THONA.

On each living thing
Hath placed his hand, and shrunk them.

SALOME.

My poor friend!

THONA.

A grisly throng strays through the courts and
ways,
Till all the city seems but an abode
Of the accursèd dead.

SALOME.

I know it, Thona.
Whilst thou hast watched beside Bernice, I
Have seen it, and I would have kept thee
here —

THONA.

And gone thyself but that we prayed thee not,
Since now fierce persecutions lie in wait
To seize upon thee, or to trace thy steps
To this our hiding-place ; for thou art known,
But here am I unknown.   Yet had I found
That which I sought, my heart had ne'er re-
    sisted
The woful looks, the fainting, fallen forms,
The outstretched hands whose skinny fingers
    spake,
The thin drawn lips which moved but uttered
    naught.

SALOME.

Ah ! it is dreadful so to see them die
Still unrepentant, helpless, hopeless people !

THONA.

Oh, it is horrible ! my heart is sick.
For frenzied creatures wander slow in groups,
And, as the starving wretches stretched their
    hands
And glared on me with eyes which seemed
    like fires
Unnatural, dull burning in dead trunks,
While from their open mouths and shrunken
    throats
They tried to utter prayers, perchance or curses,

But croaking sounds or hisses issued thence,
I shuddered; terrified, I fled — alas!
I could not help them! and they were so dread!
For they appeared as spectres mocking me,
Or who were reaching bony hands to take
And tear and slay me; and with terror faint
I neared the door; with horror still am faint
Recounting what I saw; yet what I saw
I dare not well recount; nor well could I,
For voice would fail me, hearing would fail
    thee.

SALOME.

What! worse than thou hast told?

THONA.

            The soldiers — oh!
The zealots and seditious, if perchance
Some famished beings find some nauseous thing,
Which could be eaten but when senses all
Are swallowed by insatiate sense of hunger;
Which to contemplate turns the stomach back
Recoiling on itself, ere they can gorge
Or hide the loathsome thing the soldiers seize,
Swift rushing from their vantage-ground of
    sight,
And tear it from them, from their very throats —
They cut — they do — such things I cannot
    tell.

SALOME.

Something of this I've heard, something have
  seen.
The dread Erinnyes of the Grecian stage
Are horrors not so terrible as those
Which move the personages of this scene.
We're of the chorus too. Let us endure
With patience, since naught is but by His will.
But, love, my thoughts could not go forth with
  thee,
Nor list thy dreadful tale, for they still heard
The words of sweet Bernice.

THONA.

What of her?

SALOME.

Thou know'st she prayed me to abide with her,
For she would fain confess somewhat to me.

THONA.

Repentant ever, her unsparing sight
Sees stains where others see but shadows cast.

SALOME.

She feared that she had compassed her own
  death,
And so were guilty —

THONA.

She! of her own death?

SALOME.

She thought herself more able to endure
The pains of hunger; and to spare our store
She feigned illness that she might not eat.
Her soul was stronger than her suffering flesh,
Which, overtasked, can bear its pains no more.
And, as an o'erstrained harp whose breaking
        strings
Still give forth music, so the silver chords,
Of which her life was made, in parting speak
The gentle harmony within her soul.
Though all unterrified and glad to yield,
Yet, seeing Death now entering her gates,
She fears she sinfully hath opened them
And been a traitress to the Lord of life.
Thus she, for comfort, would confess to me,
That I might aid her, were it not too late,
Against the welcome conqueror to stand,
And help her to repentance and forgiveness,
Till Duty, yielding not, but overcome,
Should render her a prisoner, and so free her.

THONA.

Her own sweet nature! thinking but for others;

2

From those she loves withholding naught, if so
She can but make them happy, or relieve them.

SALOME.

Like one a captive, ta'en in toils of war,
She yearns, calm in endurance, to be rescued.
She longs so to be free from what she calls
Her prison-house stained with impurities,
The beautiful abode in which hath dwelt
Her ever-patient spirit. She would be saved
From the corruptions which thence creep upon
Her soul; from the temptations therein coiled
To spring on it and make a cureless wound;
As serpents in the beauteous palaces,
And things malign and deadly lie concealed
In those fair countries where the genial warmth
But warms such noxious creatures into life.
And so she fears 't was not all self-denial
Which bade her suffer for us —

THONA.

Noble woman!

SALOME.

But that her selfishness hath stolen the robes,
As Selfishness oft doth, of Generousness,
And, so disguised, hath led her far astray.

THONA.

Let us go to her.

SALOME.

She is sleeping now.

THONA.

We will not wake her. Should she never wake
It were a mercy; pray that it be so.
For, waking, she must see, as must we now,
Death coming to us in so dread a form
As might appall her loving, patient spirit.

SALOME.

Remember, dear, however dark the valley,
Howe'er beset with horrors and with snares,
He leadeth us. So we are safe alike
Where Famine crawleth; where pale Pestilence
In gardens lurketh; where death-driven War
Flings conflagrations from his flaming feet;
Upon the ocean in the beaten vessel,
Or on the solid mountain's barren rocks;
In winter's tempest, or in summer's calm;
In burning deserts, or in dewy vales,
If Christ's love point the way and order us.
Let's trust in Him, and gladly, as He will,
And when He will, receive His messenger,—
Whether he come with dreadful harbingers,
The forms of violence in ghastly ranks,

The pallid, drooping banners of Disease,
Or mournful legion of the Spirit's woes,
To herald his approach; or softly come,
Unheralded, eluding every guard,
And hastening to the secret halls of life
In silence, even to the master's couch.

THONA.

And couldst thou comfort her?

SALOME.

I did, at length.

THONA.

And then she fell asleep.

SALOME.

Nay, begged us now
To leave her here, and try again to escape.

THONA.

That must we not do.

SALOME.

We must comfort her
As best we can until the Comforter
Shall lead her to His peaceful dwelling-place.
Then will we seek again a way to flee
Unto the mountains, and obey Christ's word.

The Romans hold Antonia, we'll strive
Us to surrender to them unperceived
By any of the Jews, and Sextus then, —

THONA.

Or Lepidus, mine own dear Lepidus, —

SALOME.

Who now, they say, hath brought his legion
here,
Shall give us escort safe to some asylum.

Enter CHORUS.

CHORUS.

Oh the cry! the cry
Upon the city wall!
So might a demon call
To earth and sky,
To tell the last doom nigh
And worlds appall.
They saw it while so crying, —
In form an old man horribly elate.
Like some huge pine on whose bent boughs
the weight
Of snows is lying
It stood; upon its breast and shoulders wide
Long hair and beard rolled in a snowy tide.
Of giant mould

The lofty shape, unarmed,
As some firm fortress bold,
Received the storm unharmed,
Of missiles from the cloud-like ranks
Of soldiers and of engines on the banks.
Nor could they tell,
As round him harmless arrows fell,
If that which breast and limbs defended
Were sable wings, or robes by winds distended.
And when it cried,
From every mountain side
A mocking voice replied,
Whose jeering echoes died —
List! now it crieth — Oh!

VOICE.

Woe to the city! Woe!

LEPIDUS *and* FRIGIUS.

FRIGIUS.

AH me! another tale of misery!
I thought thee happy, man. It now appears
Thou hast a plundered and a ravaged heart.
Love is a traitor, opening the gate
To admit the stealthy foe Experience,
Who crusheth every flower and verdant shrub,
Exhausts the dews, and poisons every fount,
O'ercometh Ignorance surprised, and then
Destroys his cherished treasure, happiness.
Why hast thou never spoke of this to me?

LEPIDUS.

Because I ne'er could trust to tell-tale words
The hoarded faith given unto me by her.
Nor can I prize the man who ever bears
His mistress's heart displayed upon his breast,
Not locked within; who hides not, as a miser
His precious things, the priceless proofs of love
In strongest vaults most inaccessible
Of his profoundest heart.

FRIGIUS.

Well said.

LEPIDUS.

But now,
Since, haply, in some storming enterprise
Thou shalt to Victory climb, and leave thy friend
One of the many whose strong trunks o'er-
thrown
Shall bridge the chasm for our swift-charging
hosts,
I would intrust thee with the precious casket
Where images of our true loves are shrined.
I saw her first in Germany, and —

FRIGIUS.

When?

LEPIDUS.

When I went thither on an embassy.
'T is now some five years —

FRIGIUS.

Love hath lived five years!
He must be feeble now, and in his dotage,
And cannot tell his own from other loves.

LEPIDUS.

If e'er I'm king, I'll have thee for my jester.

FRIGIUS.

To learn the truth through jests.

LEPIDUS.

But jest not now.
'T was at that tender season when the Sun
Lies wooing in the alluring lap of Earth,
The while his steeds stand still, with many a kiss
Saluting her fair cheeks —

FRIGIUS.

Oh, wicked sun !
Then his contagious fever taints men's hearts ;
His warm breath melts the humors, renders them
Combustible, does 't not ? So that the light
Shot from an ambushed eye, or briefest contact
Of glowing hands, can set them all aflame,
And their hot conflagration is called love ?

LEPIDUS.

Mayst thou be burned by it till the dull dross
Obscuring thy fine nature be consumed.
I saw her then, and from her eyes there fell
A dear enchantment on me, and soft clouds,
As they were wingèd beings sent from heaven,
Upbore me from the world where I had dwelt
To an enchanted lover's paradise,
While Love, before, with gentle dances moved.

FRIGIUS.

I fain would learn what such a place may be.

LEPIDUS.

Then must I tell thee ; there thou wilt not go.
With Love alone, as guide, the course is made,
And thou wouldst bind Love's wings and keep
    him chained,
The merest slave and drudge of merest sense.
A garden 't is, whose climate generous
Is tempered with mild incense-burning fires.
Its light is mellow, such as were this world's
If, as he near the end of his bright course,
The sun were stayed by fascinations of
Some soft-eyed evening in the blushing spring-
    time,
Till, so delaying, Jupiter in wrath
Should bar him in an alabaster tower,
Builded on mountains inaccessible
Of craggy clouds upon the western verge,
That, then, should seem a fount of pearly light.
Its breezes sweet —

FRIGIUS.

What! breezes there, and squalls,
And gales, and brooding storms, and sudden
    tempests ?

LEPIDUS.

Its breezes sweet the richest perfumes bear
From flowers sweet scented and from fruits
    exhaled,
Commingling with the odors ravishing
Which verdant April places on the robes
Of odor-loving, love-inspiring Spring.

FRIGIUS.

It must be like the shops where drugs are sold.

LEPIDUS.

Its balmy air a mystic compound is
Of sweets ethereal with magic powers,
Which plants fresh-blooming roses on the cheek,
And keeps them nurtured there; in dew em-
    balms
And guards unwithered there the modest blush,
And kindles in the eye undying light
Of warm affection, fans upon the lips
The constant glow of sweet sincerity.
Each blemish changes to perfection rich,
To comeliness every deformity.

FRIGIUS.

A place for maimed, and halt, and blind, and
    weak.
The sick should go there as to healing baths.

LEPIDUS.

Its music is the nightingale's sweet song—

PRIGIUS.

A mournful note.

LEPIDUS.

But very dear to lovers, —
Young children's voices heard in joyous sports,
And sighing tones of that most skilled musician,
The South-wind harping on the sounding vines.

FRIGIUS.

A dreadful, sense-destroying monotone.
Where is this garden ?

LEPIDUS.

It is where Love dwells,
A deity which worketh miracles.
Who from the ocean of Eternity
Doth in an instant blot the island Time,
And leaveth lovers on a raft of dreams,
To float upon the ever-blissful waves
Which gently toss, but beat upon no shore.

FRIGIUS.

I think that I should like the hard earth better.
But who is the high priestess of this god

That so dissolves the islands and o'erthrows
The natural order of the universe —

LEPIDUS.

Nay, 't is the natural order he restores.—

FRIGIUS.

And makes the senses but so many mirrors
In which Imagination sees herself?

LEPIDUS.

A captive, with a beauteous company
Of virgins in the German fastnesses
Discoverèd, who spoke our Latin tongue
Somewhat, but brokenly ; her gentle voice
By our hard letters hindered, as the breeze
By wires obstructed of the soft wind-harp,
Made sweetest music.

FRIGIUS.

Pray, what was her age ?

LEPIDUS.

Love counts not years ; he cannot calculate,
Nor knows the force of figures. She was young,
Midway 'twixt morn and noon.

FRIGIUS.

And was she fair ?

LEPIDUS.

Nor tall nor short; her dear proportions each
By manifest perfection would engage
The rest to emulation.

FRIGIUS.

What her hair?

LEPIDUS.

Such threads as rays are woven of above
The setting sun.

FRIGIUS.

Her face?

LEPIDUS.

A flowery region
Within the temperate zone, whose gentle mists
Ne'er harbored storms, but with their shadows
    made
A winning change, where else it were too bright.

FRIGIUS.

Her eyes?

LEPIDUS.

Were beds of violets which grew
Where Twilight seemed to dwell.

FRIGIUS.

Her voice?

LEPIDUS.

The music

Which chords of sympathy attuned by love
Reply to.

FRIGIUS.

Was she graceful?

LEPIDUS.

Yea, as brooklets.

FRIGIUS.

Thou art love-blind. So every lover views
His love. Gods! what a compound! Sun's
    rays, mists,
Brooks, violets, and shadows, soft wind-harps,
And flowery regions, music and — what else?
I would as lief embrace this earthy orb
And call it sweet-heart.

LEPIDUS.

Faith! I think thou wouldst.
I doubt if thou couldst find aught else to love
So well as this same world.

FRIGIUS.

Nay, be not hard.

LEPIDUS.

I will not, if thou wilt but curb thy wit.

FRIGIUS.

And the companions of this paragon.

LEPIDUS.

I knew but two. One was a Roman girl,
A princess born, who had in Britain been
A captive ; and escaping thence, by chance,
With her I loved, a British princess too,
A druid's daughter, fell into the power
Of these rapacious Germans.

FRIGIUS.

What of her?

LEPIDUS.

Young was she, yet not young; old, yet not old.
She had the dignity of two score years,
The grace of one. She had the hopeful look
Of youth, the unhopeful, patient look of age.
There was such contradiction writ on her
As spelled a mystery not well divined.

FRIGIUS.

And was she lovely too?

LEPIDUS.

As is a tree
Which blushes with delicious unplucked fruits,
While yet green leaves and blossoms deck its
boughs.
More queen than woman, goddess more than
queen,
And yet than woman still more womanly.

FRIGIUS.

What! didst thou love her too?

LEPIDUS.

I reverenced her.

FRIGIUS.

Who was the other?

LEPIDUS.

She was Jewess born,
Who had in Britain been, — I know not how,
Nor why, nor how long time, — and thence es-
    caped
With these when Plautius took the Isle of Mona,
And so chastised the druids.

FRIGIUS.

Tell her praise,
Unless thy wordy fancy hath grown tired.
Was she the porter of that Paradise,
Its evening star, its ever-changing moon,
Its Hebe, or its messenger, like Iris?

LEPIDUS.

Full beautiful she was, but very sad,
Like autumn days, ere autumn yet is old,
Which seem in sweet remembrance still to keep
The smiling, hopeful summer, and to mourn

Its end.　She chiefly loved to be alone.
If with these two, whene'er she saw me come
She would withdraw in silence.　Mourning garb
Decked her fair form.

FRIGIUS.

　　　　　　　　And didst thou reverence her?
Or worship her?　Or love?

LEPIDUS.

　　　　　　　　I pitied her.

FRIGIUS.

What was her sorrow?

LEPIDUS.

　　　　　　　　That they told me not,
But said that she bore wounds from many sorrows.

FRIGIUS.

Thou, doubtless, rescued'st them, and won thy
love,
And wearied of her.

LEPIDUS.

　　　　　　　　Nay, my plan was knit
And ready, when plot-aiding Slumber should
Its soft nets tighten round the heavy limbs
Of their custodians and hold them fast.

Ere silent Night, the dark handmaid of Slumber,
Distilled sleep-giving dews upon the world
And spread those same soft nets, a treacherous
    horde
Of sly barbarians surprised our camp,
And made me prisoner, — it is with shame
I tell it. When, by stratagem and strength,
I had escaped, I could not hear of them.
And all my search found naught but disappoint-
    ments.
Forced to return to Rome, I thence was sent,
Under Vespasian, to the Eastern wars,
And know no more of them. In vain I sought
The aid of States and interest of power.
I had but promises.

FRIGIUS.

    What were their names ?

LEPIDUS.

My dear love's name was Thona; and her
    friend's,
Salome, daughter of Herodias
The beautiful and bad.

FRIGIUS.

    What! that Salome ?
Most beautiful was she.

Her father was
That brave Antonius who went to Britain
With Plautius, there found his long-lost child,
And fell defending her. The other was
Bernice called.

FRIGIUS.

I saw Salome once.
If thou hadst loved her, I had thought thee
    wise.
Her history, they say, is very strange.
Was she still beautiful? How had she fared?
Still entertained she health like a good host?
Ruled cheerfulness or sadness in her heart?
How looked she? Smilingly? Or pale, or
    ruddy?

LEPIDUS.

Salome, then, was calm, nor gay, nor sad.
The lilies of her neck and brow and chin
Could not o'ercome the roses fast entrenched
Upon the tranquil summit of each cheek.
Upon her brow the godlike majesty
Of thought serenely sat. Beneficence,
With light benignant, circled her fair head.
And melancholy, were it there at all,
Was like a hound in godlike presence crouched.

Enter an OFFICER.

OFFICER.

The general is returned and calls for thee
In haste, Lord Lepidus.

LEPIDUS.

Any mischance?

OFFICER.

I know not what.

LEPIDUS.

I 'll come to thee again.

[*Exit* LEPIDUS.

FRIGIUS.

The general, Titus, to Antonia
This morning went with Sextus, to observe
The operations of the siege, and watch
The sallies and attacks of skirmishers.
And now he is returned in haste? Alone?

OFFICER.

Alone, my Lord, but not in haste. He came
But slowly; sad his port, and on his face
Disheveled grief lay abject.

FRIGIUS.

Canst thou guess
The cause?

OFFICER.

He went with Sextus; back he came
Alone, and, much distempered, in his tent
Sank on a chair, as if his strength of soul
Were crushed by burdens insupportable.
Unmoving, there he sits with drooping arms
And head upon his bosom, while his eyes
Are fixed on things unseen, as one whose spirit
Had left its saddened tenement to go
Some sad excursion to a distant sphere.

FRIGIUS.

To learn what's happened I will go about.
If 't be ill luck it soon will be found out.

Cæsar's Pavilion.

TITUS *and* LEPIDUS.

TITUS.

How I have pitied them and gently used
Thou knowest; now my vengeance shall have
    scope.
Ah! he was one most loving and most brave,
In whom the best of all that 's best in man
With godlike parts, strove for the mastery.
A friend most true, a most wise counselor,
Whom hope of favor, of disfavor fear
Could change not; for his course was steered
    by Truth.
And all his actions, like well-ordered ships
Móving resistless under one control
To victory, bore its fair colors ever.
He was most dear to me, as one who held
A truthful mirror to my acts and plans,
And not a portrait limned by Flattery,
To show the semblance but of what was fair.
O Sextus, Sextus, thou shalt be avenged.

LEPIDUS.

How did he fall?

TITUS.

That he was rash is true,
Or certain holy fury pressed him on.
As by Antonia's Tower we stood, to take
Observance of the works and conflict sharp
Between advance guards of our troops and those
Of these most stubborn Jews, at once appeared,
Among the Hebrew forces, one, unarmed,
On whose hard muscles Famine's rasping teeth
Had left no trace. His lofty form above
The striving foemen showed a drifted beard,
Resting like snows upon an Alpine breast.
Brightly above it, as two evil stars,
His eyes burned in the dark night of his face.
Nor spear, nor sword-thrust harmed him; on
      he came.
The Jews stood back in awe; the Romans
      paused.
Ere I could beckon Sextus to my side,
For wonder and a fearful admiration
Had held me motionless, like some foul spell,
The apparition, in a voice which seemed
From some great distance moving, called on
      him :
Ho! Sextus, ho! Ha, ha! Know'st thou me not?
Who won the game in Britain? Ho, my Sextus!
Then leaped forth Sextus with a vengeful cry,
Such as a god might give, who, searching worlds

At length beholds his foe; and sword in hand,
Rushed on the taunting monster. Then arose
A cheering shout from all the Roman host.
The Jews gave way, while his still mocking foe
Retreating, on decoyed him, till at length,
Far in advance of succor, on the stones
Which pave the Temple court, now covered
    o'er
And slippery with blood, at once assailed
Upon all sides by the returning Jews,
He slipped and fell, his armor crashing loud,
As when a cliff falls from the mountain side.
He vainly strove to rise, o'erladen now
By mounting enemies who smote him sore,
And falling foes his fatal sword o'erthrew,
And heaped upon him while himself o'erthrown.

LEPIDUS.

Could no one help him?

TITUS.

               As a beaten ship
Attacked on all sides by the gnarling waves,
When treacherous footing underneath it fails,
Goes down and disappears in sight of those
Who, powerless, stand upon the high-walled
    shore,
So sank he, and his friends could give no aid.

LEPIDUS.

Oh sad mischance! Oh loss beyond compare!
The Jews have triumphed thus in our defeat.
Yet died he gloriously as he had lived.
Now in Elysium his spirit walks,
And finds content and joy; for I have heard
That in his youth he loved as strong men
     love,
And that the frosts of chilling disappointment
Turned all that summer time of blooming hope
To wintry hopelessness; but that his soul
Was great enough to master all its ills
And hold them subject.

TITUS.

             I know all his story.
From him gushed out the noblest blood of Rome,
And sped the noblest spirit. Pure in honor,
Dishonor was to him a foreign thing,
Of which he heard, but could conceive it not
Till seen. He was a treasure-house of Justice, —
A casket where the gods kept manliness.

CHORUS *without: Roman Soldiers marching to the trenches.*

In the tent, or in the trenches,
Grappling foes or captive wenches,
Where the lance is fiercely gleaming,
Where soft eyes are mildly beaming,

Live we, pets of love and glory,
Still, when slain, to live in story.

Then joy to the soldier! A merry short life!
And luck without care in the game where he
plays,
For he's only the piece that is moved in the
strife,
While Destiny silently counts out his days, —
Who alike maketh heroes, and marshaleth gods,
Wooes dearly in Venus, in Jupiter nods.

A Chamber in Jerusalem.

MARAH.

MARAH.

ACCURSED! — O God, was there no hope for
    me
But to find credit still awhile with Death,
That he should not foreclose this tenement,
And drive my soul to wander in the storms
Of Erebus unsheltered, that I did
This most unnatural, doubly damning deed?
O God — my thoughts rise not. I cannot pray.
The weight of crime oppresseth me to hell,
And thence I cannot lift myself — O God!
God cannot hear me, for His ears are full
Of my child's cries. Oh dread! Oh murdering
    thought!
Oh torturing sense! Oh fatal memory! —
Why strive to live? Gehenna cannot hold
Fires hotter than this burning consciousness
Of ill deserts, for which hell keeps no place.
O God, upon me lay in wrath Thy finger,
And blot me out. The devils would shrink from
And leave me solitary. But why live?

For in the dread uncertainties of death
There 's naught so insupportable as life.
There's no more memory, so no more curse.
Here is its curse threefold : I cannot be
Perea's gentle, sweetly smiling beauty ;
Yet memory saith I am. It is no dream, —
I loathe the feeble thing I was, — I hate
And shudder at the loathsome thing I am,
And curse my loathing, hating, shuddering
  self.
Through memory threefold, I 'm threefold
  cursed.
Avenging conscience, hear'st thou no excuse?
Despair for him and me, frenetic pain —

JEWISH WOMEN, without.

Ah ! Oh ! Alas !
Come final woes !

MARAH.

For anguish forced me, — it was not mine act ;
My soul, benumbed, consented not unto it.

JEWISH WOMEN, without.

Ah ! Oh ! Alas !
Come fatal terror.

MARAH.

Sore hunger was upon me, yea, it held
Affection motionless in its hard gripe.

JEWISH WOMEN *without.*

Ah! Oh! Alas!
Destroy, and save us from these ravening foes!

MARAH.

No food! was dying! each day robbed and tortured
Till all was gone, and patience, and endurance.

JEWISH WOMEN, *without.*

Ah! Oh! Alas!
Consume, and save us from this racking horror.

MARAH.

One cry, *mamma;* one sigh, one look at me,
And so his life rushed into my red hand.

JEWISH WOMEN, *without.*

Accursed, ye fathers! mothers doubly cursed!
Blessed barren wombs, and breasts that never
nursed!

MARAH.

Thoughts, thoughts, ye stand devouring flames
before me.
Ye burn my brain, ye gnaw my heart away.
Help! fiends leer horribly — my bleeding child!
Help! help! I die! Not dead — not yet in hell?
Oh here is woe, woe that should break its bars.

O ribs of steel, give way; O iron heart,
Yield up the secret crimes entombed in thee.
Let every sin assume a devil's form
To jeer, and mock, and torture; range your-
    selves,
Begin your damnèd work. Oh help! Oh help!
Still, still in life? O Death, why tarriest thou?
My loathing vitals, with convulsive throes
Repel what once they bore so dearly; O God,
His sweetness on my palate turns to gall
And poison, scalding fires and lingering death.
Oh horrid, horrid feast! Oh unheard woe!
Oh last calamity of my lost people.

Enter SIMON, *with Soldiers.*

SIMON.

Now, woman, thou hast food; thou feastest.
The smell of it hath called us. Bring it forth.

SOLDIERS.

Ay, give us food.

MARAH.

Know'st thou me, Simon?

SIMON.

                        Nay.

MARAH.

Thy scent is better than thy memory.
Thou smellest out thine own, by thee forgotten.

SIMON.

Cease prating. Bring the meat.

MARAH.

Thou know'st the lambs
Grown in Perea are good ; thou 'st been there,
    Simon.

SIMON.

Perea ? What talk'st thou of Perea ?

SOLDIERS.

Flesh ! flesh !

MARAH.

I had a lamb, brought with me from Perea.

SIMON.

Let 's have it.

MARAH.

I had kept it for thee, Simon.
I loved it as a mother loves her child.
To-day I could no longer fast ; alone
I killed, cooked, ate it, Simon, — half of it.
John's soldiers would not take the rest away.
The scent hath brought thee, — dost thou know
    me, Simon ?

SIMON.

I .tell thee, nay.

SOLDIERS.

The food! the food! Bring quick
The torture.

SIMON.

Silence!

MARAH.

Patience, good my masters.
In sweet Perea lived a maid with peace.
Thou camest, Simon. When thou wentest
thence
Was sweet Perea bitter; peace had fled.
Abandoned was the maiden, and with her
A living innocent, accursed, to curse her
With thy resemblance — dost thou know me,
Simon?

SIMON.

What! Marah! No.

SOLDIERS.

Flesh! flesh! bring forth the flesh!

MARAH.

The flesh is my child, Simon — mine and thine.

SIMON.

My child!

4

SOLDIERS.

Oh horror !

MARAH.

Stay awhile — nay, stay.
Forget not thus your courtesy, my masters.
Ye start somewhat too quickly, — stay awhile.
Have ye no word to say ? Are ye afraid ?
Slink ye in silence hence ? Curs, fools, begone !
Cowards and thieves — but I 'll go with thee,
Simon.

[*Exeunt* SOLDIERS.

SIMON.

Nay, thou shalt not.

MARAH.

I will, I 'll quit thee not.
Oh let me go with thee, or stay with me.
I dare not be alone. The air is full
Of shadowy forms : young children bleeding,
ghastly,
And changing into leering demons; faces
All shapeless, growing ever still more shapeless,
And still more hideous, more mocking still,
And ever more and more like my poor child.

SIMON.

O Marah, Marah, hath it come to this ?

MARAH.

Oh leave me not. What hast thou done for me?
In that dread hour when our first mother's curse
Was doubly on me — for I, too, had eaten
Forbidden fruit with thee, and so had added
The primal curse to itself inherited —
Thou wert not there, thou did'st not comfort me.
In that great agony I was alone
With strangers, and, instead of thee, Shame stood
By me, with downcast eyes and face averted,
Her heavy finger pointing straight into
My soul, and hissed: I have so suffered,
    Simon!
Oh hide me from myself, and veil for me
With Death's dark robe the mirror of the past.
Distract me, Simon, with old vows of love.
They made me then forget all things but thee;
They may make me forget my misery.

SIMON.

Thou art beside thyself. Hence, horror, hence!
Oh thou she-Moloch, child-bane, living grave!

MARAH.

Here are the ruins of my bosom, Simon,
Which once thou thought'st so fair; two palaces,
Whose ivory domes, in thine affection glowing,

Sheltered a woman's living faith and love.
Faith was destroyed, and love hath pined away,
And so the palaces have gone to wreck.
But let thy dagger break an entrance there,
Thou 'lt find a heart still beating warm for thee
Beneath the sunken roofs; ay, Simon, let
Thy dagger enter there, and force the way
For Death. I dare not do it; when I tried
Mine arm refused; its strength, alas! was gone.

SIMON.

Take thy hands off me, snake, child-eater, swine!
I tell thee, girl, unhand me.

MARAH.

Stay with me —

SIMON.

Cease, hold me not, or I shall harm thee : hence !
I loathe thee from my soul, thou traitoress.
Thou did'st betray me when I trusted thee,
And to thine oaths of love wert ever false.

MARAH.

Oh never, Simon, ne'er, so help me Heaven, —
If Heaven vouchsafe to help me so undone, —
Did e'er a thought unworthy of thy love
Approach my heart. Thou did'st not love me,
     Simon.

SIMON.

Thou liest, girl. I loved thee as my life.
I clung to thee as the strong body clings
With all its nervous fibres to the soul,
And let thee go with as great agony.
I loved thee, girl: thou know'st not what I
  mean, —
How can'st thou know? thou so hast never
  loved.
I know not by what words to make thee feel
How thou wert of me, in me, over me,
Myself uplifted, my perfected self.

MARAH.

Oh thou could'st reckon not my love; but count
The drops of water in the sea which flows
With no receding tide, compute its mass.
Then can my love be measured; such it was.

SIMON.

Oh thou most fair outside, thou beauteous arbor
Whereon, each night, the vines and fruits of
  beauty
Hung in seductive sweetness, swaying soft,
With graceful undulations, in the breeze
Of tender passion; on which every morn
In fragrant afflorescence they appeared,
Me waking from soft slumbers with their **bloom**,

So that each day my spring and harvest was, —
My full year without winter. Oh, I 'm sick
In thinking on 't! They turned to poison when
I found another lurking in thy heart,
And thou wert proved unfaithful —

MARAH.

Never, Simon

SIMON.

Remembrance of them burns deep in my soul,
Destroying there the springs of life and hope.
Oh may each kiss I 've placed upon thy lips,
As doves upon an incense-burning altar,
Be turned to scorpions, not on thy lips,
But stinging on forever at thy heart.

MARAH.

O Simon, think on all my wretchedness,
And curse me not in this most dreadful hour.

Enter an OFFICER.

SIMON.

How now! how now? Hast thou then found
    the place
Where they conceal themselves? What is thy
    news?

OFFICER.

My Lord —

SIMON.

Speak out.

OFFICER.

I 've sought them everywhere.
Once and again have looked the palace through
In which they had been seen, but found them
not.

SIMON.

Away and search again, — look to thyself.
For if thou bring not presently report
Of where, and how, by whom she is concealed,
Thy miserable limbs in morsels torn —

OFFICER.

I 'll do my best, my Lord.

SIMON.

Thy best! What 's that?
Say thou wilt do it, wilt find her: I must have
her.
Go, go, and fail not. I must have Salome.

[*Exit* OFFICER.

MARAH.

Salome?

SIMON.

Well?

MARAH.

What wouldest thou with her?

SIMON.

What 's that to thee ?   Or, — if thou 'lt lend me
  aid,
For well I know thy strength of craftiness,
I 'll tell thee all, and, if success greet us,
Thou shalt be rich, a princess —

MARAH.

Shall I, truly ?

SIMON.

Kaliphilus, whom many now believe
One of the prophets risen from the dead,
Revealed to me that, somewhere, in the city
Salome, with a band of Christians, lurks.
That she the Jonah is whose presence here
Brings these disasters on the ship of state,
Pours all these curses on us, helps the Romans,
Turns our own arms against ourselves, and
  makes
Our contest hopeless —

MARAH.

He hath told thee this ?

SIMON.

And said that if she should be put to death,
He who should bring to pass the pious work
Should bear a crown.

MARAH.

And thou would'st win that honor?

SIMON.

In faith, would I.

MARAH.

I warn thee, Simon, lay
Not e'en a finger on that holy being.

SIMON.

Why, how now, mistress? Shall I ask thy leave
To do my pleasure? Art thou jealous, Ma-
    rah?
A plague upon thee. Go thy ways; begone!
And prate no more to me. What 's she to
    thee?

MARAH.

She sought to draw the poison from my soul,
To cure it, and to feed my famished body.
She brought God's message to a stubborn con-
    science,
But to a grateful heart —

SIMON.

Go, stand aside!
Thou art mad, — nay, stand not in my path-
    way; go.
My spies are now upon Salome's track —

MARAH.

O Simon, hast thou not yet sinned enough?
Dar'st turn and look upon the crowding crimes
Which follow thee like devils till the hour
When they shall fall upon, and drag thee down
To punishment, and night, and burning tortures,
Repentance hopeless, and remorse eternal?
Oh add not to their number this so great.
Oh spare Salome; nay, protect her too,
And it shall be remembered for thy good.

SIMON.

I tell thee, girl, Kaliphilus hath said
That, whether judged by Christian or by Jew,
Salome should by either be condemned:
By Christian, for she murdered John the Bap-
tist;
By Jew, for she's a Christian and blasphem-
eth.

Enter KALIPHILUS.

MARAH.

I care not what Kaliphilus may say.
I know him not; he is some plotting knave.
I'll tell her of her peril, find a — ah!

KALIPHILUS.

God's curse upon thee, woman, if thou help her.
A leprosy consume thy false outside,

And turn thy walls to chalk; gaunt Famine
gnaw
Forever on with unrelenting teeth,
And suck the marrow from thy shrunken bones;
Thirst build its fires upon thy swollen tongue,
And keep them burning never to be quenched;
Hot fevers dry the sluiceways of thy body,
And leave them gaping; dread Delirium hold
Thy crimes in full deformity, like fiends,
To thine appalled gaze; Remorse in frenzy
Pursue thee, shrieking; be thy soul on fire,
And every nerve an instrument of torture;
Despair pull at thy heart-strings toward the
gulf,
And all her furies haunt thee while thou wakest;
Let Hell surround and press upon thee sleeping,
And Death avoid thee, howsoe'er besought:
Such be thy doom if thou shalt dare to aid
One upon whom God's curse hath once been
laid,
Or if thou aid not, so as best thou can
To punish one who lies beneath His ban.

[*Exit* KALIPHILUS.

SIMON.

Well may'st thou tremble, girl.

MARAH.

Oh! I am faint!

What shall I do? O Simon, leave me not.
Who was that dreadful being? Whence came
    he?

SIMON.

He was Kaliphilus, who having learned
That I was here, from some one, hither came
To seek me, doubtless; or his wondrous power
Informed him where I was, and what I would,
And so he came —

MARAH.

        Oh go not with him, Simon.
But stay a little with me, stay a little.
He is no angel, — nay, nay, trust him not.

SIMON.

If I by staying win thee to make known
Salome's hiding-place, I then will own
The time well spent.

MARAH.

        Am I, then, naught to thee?
For what I 've done wilt thou do naught for
    me?
As I have helped thee sinning, — come with-
    in, —
Oh now so let me help thee not to sin.

A Tent near Cæsar's Pavilion.

LEPIDUS, FRIGIUS, *and other* OFFICER.

LEPIDUS.

THIS wine was grown on Horace's old farm.
Would he were here to drink it.

FRIGIUS.

That he were!
'T would do me good to hear him laugh at thee,
A love-sick soldier, yet a brave one too.

LEPIDUS.

But he is drinking nectar with the gods.
If I be brave I should be true in love,
And tender my affection tenderly,
For bravery is one half tenderness.
The men of courage aye are men of heart,
And men of heart must aye love constantly,
And constancy, when crossed by disappoint-
     ments,
Is an unhealing wound; the whole man thence
Is fired with fever, and grows rash and fierce.
As thou art brave, come, pledge me once to her,
The love I lost —

FRIGIUS.

The lost whom thou dost love.

LEPIDUS.

The one I mourn —

FRIGIUS.

The mourner thou had'st won.

LEPIDUS.

The god of love, by thine impiety
To him, offended, shall yet punish thee;
And when he smites thee for thy heartless
    jeers,
Thy heart shall toss upon a flood of tears.

FRIGIUS.

Who knows? It may be in Elysium
That we shall, all together, pledge again.
So cheer up, man; give us a merry song, —
He used to sing as if a Muse had borne
    him, —
A tripping measure, one to stir the blood,
And dull thy wits no more with memories.

LEPIDUS.

I cannot sing, for all things are ajar,
And e'en celestial harmony would mar.

An accident hath made all things go wrong,
All out of tune, and so would be my song.

FRIGIUS.

It is thyself who now art out of tune,
Discordant with all things beneath the moon.
So might a harp-string fallen from its strain
That all the strings were out of tune complain.
But sing —

ALL.

Ay, sing, whate'er thou wilt, but sing.

LEPIDUS.

One of my own, a little, simple thing.

[*Sings.*

Zephyr, come, come by.
  Hast thou seen my dear?
Bringest thou her sigh
  To me here?

Breathèd she a name
  When she sighed, my fair?
Ah! was it the same
  Which I bear?

Are thy soft wings wet
  With her falling tears?
Fall they for me yet
  Spite of years?

To her now return,
　Tell my long-lost dove
How for her I mourn,
　How I love.

FRIGIUS.

Gay ! —

FIRST OFFICER

Tripping measure ! —

SECOND OFFICER.

Stirring up the blood !

FRIGIUS.

As warm as falling snow-flakes —

THIRD OFFICER

Twice as tender —

SECOND OFFICER.

And airy : tell us, went the Zephyr back ?

LEPIDUS.

The song was gay since it hath moved your
　laughter,
And stirred the blood which warms your ready
　wit.
Now Frigius will sing a merry song, —
One that he calleth merry.

ALL.

Frigius!

FRIGIUS.

I 'll do my best, if you will join the chorus.

ALL.

Agreed: what is 't?

FRIGIUS.

You 'll catch it on the wing.

[*Sings.*

A friend and a flagon of wine well filled,
And a wench in the dance and in music well
    skilled
  To amuse, and, perchance, to deceive me;
Who laugheth at Love and his sorrowful train,
Who never is sad, and will never complain,
  Are the joys of my life, sirs, believe me.

CHORUS.

To Friendship and Venus we 'll drink then, and
    sing
Ho, ho for the kingdom where Bacchus is
    king!
We 'll mount on the fumes of the wine and
    away —
To-morrow ne'er cometh, our life is to-day.

5

The gods are the jolliest fellows alive,
Ne'er sighing for love, never wishing to wive,
   They shake Olympus with laughter.
With very best nectar their bowls overflow,
They care not what happens above or below,
   And think not what may be hereafter.

CHORUS.

To Friendship and Venus we 'll drink then, and
   sing
Ho, ho for the kingdom where Bacchus is king!
We 'll mount on the fumes of the wine and
   away —
To-morrow ne'er cometh, our life is to-day.

We cannot be gods. Let us like the gods be,
And woo every beautiful woman we see, —
   In Protean forms swear we love her.
Ne'er loving, and sure, when all other forms
   fail,
There is one that hath always, and aye shall
   prevail, —
   The golden shower above her.

CHORUS.

To Friendship and Venus we 'll drink then, and
   sing
Ho, ho for the kingdom where Bacchus is king!

We 'll mount on the fumes of the wine and
    away —
To-morrow ne'er cometh, our life is to-day.

FIRST OFFICER.

Good! That becomes a man.

THIRD OFFICER.

                    Faith! Excellent.

SECOND OFFICER.

A brave song, Frigius, and bravely sung.

LEPIDUS.

'T is pity when sweet music is profaned
By impious verse, — a thousand times more pity
Than to see Venus in the arms of Vulcan.

FIRST OFFICER.

We have o'erstayed our time, our duties call.

LEPIDUS.

Then will I keep you not. Accept my thanks
For courteous company, and my excuse
That I cannot be merry as yourselves.

FIRST OFFICER.

We are thy debtors till we meet again.
                 [Exeunt all but LEPIDUS *and* FRIGIUS.

FRIGIUS.

Now is the time, and I am in the mood,
Although thou thinkest not, to hear thy story.
That powerful love of thine who gently bore,
Like Atlas young, a new world on her shoulders,
And thee within it, did she weary grow,
And cast it —

LEPIDUS.

She could never weary grow
Of her own lovely self, my world of love.

FRIGIUS.

And leave thee, Alexander-like, to weep
For some new world to conquer?

LEPIDUS.

No new world,
Though peopled with the fairest goddesses
That e'er wore woman's form, displayed her
charms,
By her enticements made men madly fall,
Or made them heroes passing demi-gods,
Could turn my thoughts from the dear one I
love,
Though it were blasted, or I banished thence.

FRIGIUS.

Be blind and see no other bliss but this,

Her sighs, her yearnings, tender words, hot
    tears,
Heart-palpitations, bosom-heaving sobs,
Smoth'ring embraces, seeming perfect trust,
Abandonment of her whole self to thee,
Which she would make appear oblivious, —
Oh blissful dreamer, dreaming of such bliss,
And cursed because thy blissful dream is this.

LEPIDUS.

It is no dream ; Love maketh all bliss real,
Imagination may, as dreams, conceive —

FRIGIUS.

Invests a clown with graces from the skies,
Endues a fool with wisdom of the gods,
An Ethiop clothes in Iris, shining robes :
Go on with the true tale of thy true love.
If I can help prolong this dream I will,
Since 't is thy fancy to be happy thus.
I 'll give thee sleeping draughts, love potions,
    keep
Disturbance hence, or strive to master it,
Should it approach in form of some fair woman.
Now, look at me, I 'm solemn as thyself.

LEPIDUS.

When some great bird of sorrow, darkening
    heaven,

Shall cow thy soul which crows so lustily,
'T will seek, with drooping plumage, head low
    bent,
The shelter of sweet sympathy, content.

FRIGIUS.

Nay, tell me in good sooth and sympathy
Of all thy love for her, and hers for thee.
Or, shall I con it in some poet old?
I trow such tales have oft before been told.
The names and actors change, but still the play
Is played in words unchanging day by day.
Now am I serious, employ my mood,
And, by imparting, give thy love its food.

LEPIDUS.

I would Experience might teach thee how
Love may be true, and sacred keep its vow;
Then should'st thou reverence what thou now
    dost rate
The cheat of knaves and folly of the great.

FRIGIUS.

When sweet Experience shall teach me this,
May I be skilled to call such learning bliss.

LEPIDUS.

With the barbarians in Germany
My love, and her companions —

FRIGIUS.

Were as trees
Transplanted to base uses, fading there —

LEPIDUS.

Nay, were as plants walled in and sacred held
For healing virtues. On their way from Britain,
Driven on that frigid coast and taken captive,
Salome, and the others, all were brought
Before the chief, who, then, the subject was
Of powerful maladies, whose secret wiles
His doctors, ignorant, could not defeat.
Salome, by a power these Christians have,
When holy as herself, laid skillful siege,
And shortly made Disease capitulate.
The chief set free, and to his realm restored,
In grateful health proclaimed at once a law
Which made their persons sacred, and thence-
    forth
None, save his gods, with him had so much
    worth.

FRIGIUS.

So then, thy love is a wise woman's pupil,
And in that forest shade, ere this, no doubt,
Hath instituted an academy.
There shalt thou find her teaching youthful
    Germans,
And giving them the name of Thonians.

For no such manly work was she inclined,
Yet for good actions ever had a mind.

FRIGIUS.

Salome, there, could follow out her bent,
And lecture gaping men-wives in a tent.

LEPIDUS.

The gods ne'er saw, with their far-reaching
    gaze,
A modesty more excellent than hers,
A gentleness more gentle, heart more full
Of ready sympathy. Her life was worth,
In her esteem, the good she did, no more.
Such as she was, such was my Thona too.
And, under guidance of sweet Charity,
They sought out woes with such timidity
That thou wouldst say they were almost ashamed
To be encountered as the followers
Of this fair mistress, lest it should appear
They followed her too poorly. Where they
    went,
To meet them tearful thanks and prayers were
    sent.

FRIGIUS.

They made a progress very April-like.

LEPIDUS.

Their frank but modest look, their soft dis-
      course,
Their gentle bearing, their chaste courtesy
Was but their beauty in harmonious action, —
A guard of powerful charms repelling all
Too venturous thoughts, or over-bold desires.
And timorous sense of woman's winning weak-
      ness
With magic weapons furnished loveliness,
And gave an air entreating to their grace,
Whose every action seemed to ask protection.
And guardian Innocence invested them
With majesty 'fore which the boldest words
Were dumb; with certain trustfulness which
      pleaded,
And which, in woman's mien, ne'er fails to
      rouse
The noblest feelings of the noblest men,
And gentleness create in breasts the rudest.

FRIGIUS.

Lo, I grow gentle hearing thee relate.
Had I but seen them it had made me great.

LEPIDUS.

Their presence was like Music when she moves
Enchanting passions base to helplessness,

And freeing the diviner parts in man
By these same passions tyrannous oppressed.

FRIGIUS.

But did'st thou tell thy love ?   And loved she
   too ?

LEPIDUS.

One day when Phœbus' ardent eye had driven
The lolling kine to shelter of deep shade,
And men had hidden from his majesty,
As they had feared the god in his bright pres-
   ence,
I sought a brook which, for its dainty course,
Had paved a way with white and moss-grown
   stones
And work Mosaic made of varied pebbles,
O'er which it sauntered in the coolest bowers
Of overhanging trees and blooming shrubs.
There, seated on a happy bank, was she, —
One little foot half-buried in the stream,
Which tarried, gurgling, round the pretty thing,
And stretched its lips to kiss the ankle white.
Her hair, unbound, adown her shoulders fell,
And o'er her bosom as it were the wings
Of some bright angel guarding Innocence.
Her robe undone, that she might lave her throat,
Displayed her fair round neck —

FRIGIUS.

And beauties there
Like rose-buds white just bursting from their
husks.

LEPIDUS.

I would escape unseen to fright her not.
But, ere I could withdraw, the sentinels
Placed at the roseate gateways of her soul,
O'er which her tresses, as luxuriant vines,
Hung, half concealing them, gave warning.
Then
She started up, and, seeing me, a blush
Changed noonday fair to evening's lovelier hue
In that sweet heaven on which my gaze was
fixed,
As, with eyes downcast, trembling, eager hands
She tried, unskillfully to hide those charms.

FRIGIUS.

And skillfully thou did'st assail her then,
To gain possession of them ta'en by storm.

LEPIDUS.

With reverence, such as at the holiest shrine
Pleads for the worshiper, who there would seek
The oracle in which his life is summed,
I neared her ; and as best my heart could speak,
Avowed my love and pleaded for her own.

She shook with gentle terror, turned her face,
Suffused like morning, from me, while her hand
Strove to be free more like a timid thing
Than one in anger —

FRIGIUS.

     And thou thoughtest real
This coyness counterfeit?

LEPIDUS.

      Into mine arms
And to my breast with gentle force I drew her,
And there she panted as she would inhale
A breath of life immortal passing near,
And live forever. Then I bent my head
And gathered unripe kisses, not yet bloomed,
But sweet as dewy rose-buds on her lips.
Still only half-concealed were those twin altars
Of whitest alabaster, on whose summits
The constant fires of love glow constantly.
Her perfect form had made a Grecian worship.

FPIGIUS.

Fie! Lepidus! I pray thee talk not so.
Destroy not all those flowers of modesty,
My blushes, with such overheated words.
The delicacy of my soul should be
Still unimpaired by any word of sense.

LEPIDUS.

A madcap art thou. What! art grown so nice
In this o erscrupulous age, so deeply skilled
In hidden knowledge, that no word of love
But to its ear a hidden meaning gives,
Which makes it think it ought to blush, yet
 cannot?
No name which shows distinguishment of sex
But it would shun, as showing guilty knowledge.
E'en in the closet must no word be spoke
Describing beauties all the world may see.
No name of image or of aught pertaining
To Love's delightful worship but their souls,
Whose empty voices make the loud'st outcry,
Submerged in sense till they are sensual all,
Perceive what brings them shame. Yet they
 unveil
Those sacred altars in Love's holiest shrine
To vulgar and profane; and still the nearest
Shall but offend if by a word he show
That he sees aught, or worships what is seen,
As Beauty aye is worshiped by the pure.
For, knowing naught, in this all-sensual mood,
But Love profaned, they may not comprehend
That Love and Beauty are a wedded pair,
And Poetry their first-begotten child,
Who, uncorrupted, speaketh guilelessly
As children speak; and loveth that the most
To Love and Beauty equally most dear.

FRIGIUS.

Ah! then 't is thou art Poetry uncorrupted.
Thou speakest guilelessly as children speak.
Oh! thus I 'm in no danger; pray go on.

LEPIDUS.

Should Venus' priestesses be all debased,
Profaned by them her pure, primeval worship,
The purest worshiper in formal words
Should, in their vision, be as vile as they.

FRIGIUS

Nay, talk of love. I hate philosophy.
We left thee with thy loved one in thine arms.

LEPIDUS.

Still pleading for her love, some word, some
    sign;
Her bosom heaved against my rib-bound heart
Like tides of ocean on the rocky flanks
Of some volcano shaken by its fires —

FRIGIUS.

Or ruddy apples tossed upon a brook.

LEPIDUS.

Peace, mocker! peace! What! Shall I beat
    thee?

FRIGIUS.

Nay.
I pray thee do not, for the mad are strong.
I would but aid thee with comparisons.
What proofs would'st thou have more? Wert
  thou content?

LEPIDUS.

Ay, almost sad with great excess of joy,
For as I loved her so did she love me.
And, till the treacherous villains spoiled my
  plot,
Which should have knit our destinies for aye,
This love grew hourly and suffused our souls.
But so to leave her, no long farewells said,
No last kiss, knowing it to be the last,
In whose dear agony half of each soul
Torn from itself is to the other given
In pledge eternal of eternal love!—
Oh could I hold her in my arms again
But for one moment, or the hundredth part
Of time's minutest measure, I would give
The rest of life, if such the forfeit were,
And die in ecstasy, this longing ended.

Enter a SOLDIER.

SOLDIER.

My Lord, I bear a message; here 't is writ.

LEPIDUS. (*Reads.*)

To the great generals Lepidus or Sextus.
Whence had'st thou this, my man?

SOLDIER.

                                A personage
Who might have been a messenger from Hades,
Or from supernal gods, so dread his mien,
Appeared before, and gave this letter to me.

LEPIDUS.

What was he like?

SOLDIER.

                        A man; and yet unlike.
His eyes were as two fires; his voice was heard
As might be moanings of some mighty shade,
Disconsolate, when wafted o'er the Styx.

FRIGIUS.

This soldier is a poet. He hath seen
A starveling Jew, and his poetic vision
Conceived a wonder: magnified his bones
Till they were frame-work for a universe;
Saw each dull orb a world in conflagration;
Heard the dread din of Hades from his mouth,
And—speaketh guilelessly as children speak—
A plague on all the race! of use to none:

Full of untruths, they history pervert;
Full of presumption, Nature they distort,
All, — thee excepted, Lepidus, my friend.
But read the letter, pray let's know his news.

LEPIDUS. (*Reads.*)

Salome and Thona are in the city, starving!
Shame! idlers, craven Romans, lovers false!
Starving!

FRIGIUS.

Salome and Thona in the city!

LEPIDUS.

Impossible —

FRIGIUS.

Can it be true?

LEPIDUS.

If so,
With one blow he hath given me life and death.

FRIGIUS.

Whence came this messenger?

SOLDIER.

I cannot tell.
I saw him not till he accosted me.

LEPIDUS.

My Thona here, so near me? Lover false!
Ay false, who could not feel her holy presence,
If she indeed be here. Yet how to prove it?

FRIGIUS.

But whither went he?

SOLDIER.

Toward the city gate —

FRIGIUS.

Untouched?

SOLDIER.

Ay, though our soldiers smote at him,
And thrust with spears, and flung their javelins,
Which turned aside as they had glanced from
     shields
Invisible, and arrows flew astray
About him, turning not, until he vanished.

LEPIDUS.

He vanished!

SOLDIER.

Ay, my Lord, he disappeared
As he had sunk into the solid earth.

LEPIDUS.

When was this?

SOLDIER.

Early in the morning watch,
Ere yet the torch of Dawn had lit the world.

LEPIDUS.

Why comest thou so late?

SOLDIER.

At first, my Lord,
I could not leave my post, and when relieved,
I hastened straightway to the tent of Sextus,
Who then with Titus had to Antonia gone.
I sought thee in thy tent; thou, too, wert forth
Upon some secret duty; none could say
Where I might find thee.

LEPIDUS.

It is well. Retire.

[*Exit* SOLDIER.

FRIGIUS.

A strange tale, truly.

LEPIDUS.

Yet the man is brave,
And fears nor shade nor demon. Counsel me.

84 SALOME.

FRIGIUS.

I would to Titus, make the matter known,
And seek his aid. Josephus, too, perchance,
The wise man of the Jews, could counsel thee.
Demand a parley, question then the Jews —

LEPIDUS.

Thou sayest well. If this be aught but sound,
Or Lepidus is lost or Thona found.

KALIPHILUS.

YET they are here. Of that my skill assures me,
Which, like a woman, hath me hither led
To balk me now that I would grasp the prize.
For two whole days, two sleepless nights, I 've
    sought,
By every crafty instrument of power,
To find their lurking-place, without avail.
In vain I 've studied till I can outdo
My masters, as could Moses. I have gone
Beyond the bounds of knowledge, and have found
Such skill and potency in use of Nature
That magic is a shallow trickster's art
Compared with master secrets in my power,
Which guide me to the hidden treasure-house,
But mock me now that I would have the key :
Yet are they here, and I must find them out.
I turn to you, O dwellers in the heart:
Ye shall not fail me ; answer to my skill,
And by you shall I yet achieve my will.
Now have I Sextus ; Lepidus, ere this,
Hath read my message, and, to save his love,

Some desperate move shall make, and I will
    take him.
If he do not, why, then I need him not,
Since I have taken Sextus in my plot.
With these I bait the traps for those; with
    those
For these, who shall, for love, themselves dis-
    close.
And, when the covert is discovered, then,
O God-defying Stubbornness, stand firm,
And give no ground to swift and sharp accusers.
Yet dare I not look on my crime marked out
In plain and definite words; its aspect dread
Would, as a Gorgon's, turn me into stone,
But for my doom which holds this solid flesh
Unchangeable, this warm blood uncongealed,
Yet must confront it. Let me be the thing
This doom hath made me, seeking not to thwart
The purpose of the Infinite, ha, ha!
For he that is accursed a curse must be.
Let me be great in it, as Satan great,
Ay, overdo his cunning and his hate.

Enter SIMON.

Have they been found?

SIMON.

Nay —

KALIPHILUS.

Marah aids thee not?

SIMON.

Not yet.   Perchance —

KALIPHILUS.

The torture might induce her.

SIMON.

I would not use it; know, she is my wife.

KALIPHILUS.

Hath been so racked and buffeted by thee
She would not mind the torture; thou art right.
But it concerns thee to find out these Christians,
If thou would'st save the city and be king.
Look to it well.   To me it matters not.
This nation rusheth howling, shrieking down
To silent, desolate, and final ruin.
But, as a vessel shivered by the lightning,
It leaveth me afloat, to beat all shores,
Yet ne'er to find the thing thou dread'st, a
        grave.
What are to me these flames and falling towers?
I cannot perish.   So shall I see fall,
As 't were, from year to year, the leaves and
    .   fruit,

Cities and nations from the world's old tree,
With ripeness heavy in the age's autumn,
As cycle followeth cycle till the end;
Or blighted in their green and crescent state,
And scattered by the storm-breath of the Al-
    mighty,
Which maketh winter in the universe.
I, as an angel, see them go, and hear
Ravage of cities and the rush of ruins,
As man the rustle of the falling leaves.
Henceforward I 've no country. In each land
A phantom from the shadows of the past
Shall I appear; and in each prosperous nation,
As on a ship, in pleasant weather, sail
The space that lies 'twixt the dim shores of ages.
When cometh a fierce storm, I 'll leave the vessel
To those who own it; let them struggle for it,
And save it, if they can.

SIMON.

                    Since thou permittest
Thy servant to hear so much of thyself,
Vouchsafe, I pray, to tell me who thou art.

KALIPHILUS.

One who can aid thee, if thou wilt obey.

SIMON.

I will obey in all things possible.

KALIPHILUS.

Things possible! 'T is well. Go to my dwell-
ing,
There shalt thou find the Roman general
Sextus.

SIMON.

How! Is he —

KALIPHILUS.

Hence, and do as I command,
And bear him thence into the castle dungeon.
Then cause a proclamation to be made
That Sextus is a prisoner in the castle,
And that he shall be crucified to-morrow.

SIMON.

It shall be done. And then?

KALIPHILUS.

I 'll tell thee more.
[*Exit* SIMON.

She surely shall the proclamation hear,
Or some kind friend shall tell it in her ear.
Forgetful of all caution, she will flee
To Sextus in his dungeon — that 's to me.
The net is set, and placed is the decoy,
The dove will fly into the snare with joy.

A Chamber in Jerusalem.

SALOME, THONA, *and* BERNICE.

BERNICE, *waking.*

WILL he not come ? Oh ! will he never come ?
I loved him so — he hath forgotten me.
But he hath gone away, and never more
May come to stay my weeping as of yore.

SALOME.

Bernice, dear.

BERNICE.

　　　　　Ah ! thou art here, Salome,
My loved protectress, my dear guide to hope.
I ne'er can tell the gratitude I owe
To thee, and to the Tenderness which sent thee.

SALOME.

How art thou, love?

BERNICE.

　　　　　Almost well, almost well.
I have been dreaming of the olden time,

Of one I loved — my thoughts will cling to
    earth ;
In sleep I seemed to live earth's sorrows o'er.

SALOME.

The constant heart loves constantly till death,
Oft clings to the unworthy and the vile,
As vines still cling, e'en when their leaves have
    fallen,
To branches all decayed and trunks polluted.

BERNICE.

Oh is it wrong in this most solemn hour,
While I can see, as 't were, the messengers
Sent to conduct me to our Father's house,
By Love and Condescension infinite,
And feel myself almost in heavenly presence,
For me to think upon Kaliphilus?

SALOME.

Ah me! I cannot deem it wrong to love.

BERNICE.

Oh that he could be brought from wandering!
That I could see him once and plead with him
To bow his pride, and feel the sad, sweet joy
Of penitence, and ever present bliss
Of full forgiveness. How I pity him!
How mournful is his case! How very dreadful!

SALOME.

Even for him there may be mercy yet.

BERNICE.

O tell him, for thou yet, perchance, shall see
    him,
That, till my death, I prayed for him ; that still,
If after death it be permitted me,
My soul shall wrestle for his poor soul's weal.
And tell him that — if it may comfort him —
I loved him still, — with pure and chastened
    love,
As I dare trust. Beseech him to repent.
Wilt thou do this for me ?

SALOME.

              I will, I will.

BERNICE.

Salome, take my hand, and yield it not,
Save to the heavenly guides who wait for me.
As thou didst lead me from the ways of sin
Conduct me so unto the gate of heaven.
Farewell, dear Thona. Thou hast not dis-
    dained
To be to me a sister. Fare thee well.
Give my last greetings to the faithful band
Who with us have so long been sorely tried.
Do not let go my hands. I fain would sleep.

CHORUS, *Christians in another chamber.*

God is our refuge, ever present aid,
Our firm foundation ere the worlds were made.
Therefore we fear not, though the earth remove,
And roll away in flames the skies above.

Though all the nations rage and be our foes,
Though hell let loose on us infernal woes,
Though seas mount up on seas and reach to
    heaven,
Though day in night be lost, and morn in even,

Though utter darkness reign in utter space,
Though Death in hideous form hold every place,
Though chaos in the centre whelm the pole,
And dread confusion through creation roll,

Though nether regions be commixed with
    heaven,
And all the stars be from their stations riven,
God is our refuge, our unfailing strength,
And mercy, silent long, will speak at length.

BERNICE.

At home! dear home! Do ye not see the hills
Which guard our own dear valley? though I
walk —

Though I walk through the valley — see ! the
tents —
The flow'rets sweet which blossom in the meadows.

THONA.

She is not well asleep.

SALOME.

Perchance her soul
Is breaking free to visit the loved spots
Of earth before it takes a final flight.

BERNICE.

I have so longed to see my native hills —
From whence cometh my help, — I will lift
up —
'T is gone — I cannot find it. See ! they 're
armed !
Their russet armor glances through the rents
Of mantles battle-torn — and when he called
They came and helped him, — giant men-at-
arms.
They fear no foe, and — they are resting now —
Lo ! he is coming ! he is on the hills !
I 'll go to meet him. Oh ! are they not fair ?

SALOME.

She feels no pain. She shall not suffer more.

BERNICE.

Who called me ? Ah ! I 'll come, I 'll come,
  I hear.
Leave me a little while — it is so fair —
And now the lambs are coming to the fold.

THONA.

Alas ! alas ! Will she not know us more ?

SALOME.

Yea, let us hope so, in the blessèd mansions.

BERNICE.

O mother ! mother ! I have come again.
Forgive me, mother. Ah ! she hears me not.
The sky is over them — and in its place
The sun goes up and down — and gentle clouds,
Behold those gentle clouds ! — how beautiful !
They wing the air and come beneath the sun —
The saints redeemed, in white below the Throne
Are gathered — now they bow themselves in
  praise —
Are they not saints ? How white and pure they
  are !
Are they not saints ? Who told me they were
  saints ?

THONA.

So white and pure shalt thou be, blissful saint.

Enter CHORUS.

SALOME.

Well come, dear friends, in time to see our
loved one
Depart before us to a better country.

CHORUS.

The guest is ready, with her wedding garments
on.
Her longings shall be ended in fruition full.
And wooed no more by sins in angel forms, no
more
Must she, with sleepless penitence the live-long
night,
Undo in tears the web of errors wrought by day.
No more shall trials crush her down with moun-
tain weight.
Reposing ever in His house, upon His breast
Shall she, in trust eternal, find eternal rest.

BERNICE.

They melt away! they fade! they fade! alas!
I cannot see them more.

SALOME.

The shadow falls.

BERNICE.

Only the clouds — the fair white clouds — they
come!

THONA.

She is, perchance, entranced. It is a vision.

CHORUS.

He 'll bring her to His Father's palace,
Whose portico is built of planets,
And He shall lead her to the gardens.
No tempests and no storms can come there,
Nor war's alarms, nor sound of battles.
There are no lightnings, there no thunders;
Shut thence, they hiss and roar in Hades,
Or haunt, with storms, the earth to threaten.
And, driven out by Love, Fear hideth
With men, and Hate with demons dwelleth.

BERNICE.

Lo! over them the sky hath gone away!
Oh! Oh! How wonderful! How beautiful!

CHORUS.

And by the river,
Where bloometh evermore,
In groves soft breathing,
The eternal tree of life,
Shall He conduct her,
And lead her by the hand.
The mantle of His love
Shall cover her securely.
7

She shall repose in bliss,
And never more be weary.

SALOME.

My love, what dost thou see?

THONA.

She heeds thee not.

CHORUS.

And there shall she be crowned with glory,
And Joy shall shout from all the arches,
And Love's sweet essence, Trust, shall guard
    her,
And heavenly Peace shall be her pillow.
She shall go no more out forever,
Nor ever more be grieved or anxious.
She shall no more remember sorrow,
But, with infinity of blessing,
Within His arms, upon His breast,
Forever and forever rest.

BERNICE.

They come! — the clouds! Ah! No, they are
    not clouds,
But angels — and the glory over them —
They stretch their arms to me — I cannot lift
My hands. O blissful Beauty! Love! O Life!

[*Dies.*

Ended the night, the morning appeareth.
Leaving the body, which pressed, as a night-
mare,
Trooping temptations and sins, and accusals,
Down on the spirit enthralled and in anguish,
Goeth she now to be bathed in the glory,
Robed with the righteousness, crowned with
the beauty
Of the slain Lamb, the Christ, the Redeemer.
So the Eternal day for her beginneth.

A Mountain overlooking Jerusalem.

TITUS *and* JOSEPHUS.

JOSEPHUS.

THY purpose gained, and all the city viewed
From this high place, I pray thee grant me
    leave
To stay a little here ; and pardon me
Some natural weakness, as, for the last time,
I gaze upon that city and that Temple.
Unfaithful deem me not.

TITUS.

                Mourn not too much
Thy country's ruin.   Seek to know the will
Of thine own God, whom I, too, venerate.

[*Exit* TITUS.

JOSEPHUS.

O thou beleaguered city ! O thou queen
Disrobed, imprisoned, scourged, defiled, in
    chains,
Mine eyes will not behold thee ; veiling mists
Are drawn before their wounded vision ; tears

Dissolve thy burning image in my brain.
O Zion, loved of David, O thou bride
Of Israel, the heathen have unloosed
Thy girdle, and have gazed upon thy beauty.
Their arms encompassed thee, they have de-
    spoiled thee.
For thou didst wanton with them, and thine
    eyes
Went softly after them; thy smiles invited.
Thou yearnèdst for their love; thy lips con-
    fessed it.
Thou madest bare thy breasts; thy shining
    feet
Strayed in their paths; thy white hands beck-
    oned them;
Thy voice, in sighing accents, sang of love.
Thy spoilers have been many; thou hast thought
Them lovers, but they were thy masters; now
They cast thee off to be the scorn of nations.
Oh woe is me for thee, beleaguered city!
Oh woe is me for thee, thou bride of Israel!
Thou God of Abraham, if it be meet
Thy servant should Thine awful purpose know,
O condescend, from Thy dread Dwelling Place,
To send Thy messengers, and Thy decree
Reveal, O Holy One, if it may be.
Thine answering thunders rush along the sky;
In dread expectance on my face I lie.

102

Enter an OFFICER.

OFFICER.

My Lord —

JOSEPHUS.

How now ? What ? would the general march ?

OFFICER.

He sent me not, — but please thee now move **on.**
The sun, like an empyreal ship aflame
On an empyreal ocean, goeth down
Far from the shore of the blue firmament.
The clouds, like waves white crested, black be-
        neath,
Surge round him with tempestuous turning tides.
The earth lies still with awe. The valley 's dim,
Already, with the slowly moving shadows,
Night's escort, marching up the mountain side,
With banners gold and scarlet in mid heavens,
To seat her on its crest. The sky, o'erhead,
Is clear; yet is there something in the air
More terrible than storms. The camels look
With frightened gaze toward heaven and snuff
        the breeze,
With terror trembling, uttering the cry
With which they greet the yet far off Simoom.
The dogs crouch low and whine ; the horses
        snort,
Toss high their upright manes, with eyes aflame,

And, hungry as they are, refuse to eat.
Oh let us go; I pray thee, let us go.

JOSEPHUS.

Hast thou heard aught?

OFFICER.

Yea, I have heard, my Lord,
The distant rushing sound of many wings,
The heavy thunder — now again it rolls! —

JOSEPHUS.

Return unto thy post, and there await
The general's orders.

[*Exit* OFFICER.

Lord, upon my face,
If I, so mean, may find with Thee such grace,
Grant unto me to know Thy holy will.
In midst of wrath remember mercy still.

A VOICE *from the far heights.*

Amen!
Patience cease.
Vengeance call thy chiefs.
Send the winds to fetch last plagues;
Set them on this people; on their heads
Horrors pour; madden them with woe.
In their hearts let miseries nest.
Every curse exhaust.
Do thy worst.
Amen!

104

Josephus! What! Josephus, come away.

JOSEPHUS.

The Lord hath spoken. Let the Earth keep
silence.

Voice of Vengeance, *descending.*

On, Discord! In the van of all thy force
Place Jealousy, Ambition, Envy, Pride.
Enrage this nation. All thy terrors move.
Let thy fell imprecations fill the air.
Tear from the North the South, from East the
West.
Thy breast by thine own hands be riven ;
thence
Let tainting vapors every eye infest,
That, with distorted vision, they behold
No friends, all enemies, and all assail.
Let thy hot breath enflame each soul with hate.

Phantom of Discord, *rising.*

Ay, I have so unstrung their polity
It sounds but dissonance. Now it shall grate,
And, of itself, scream anarchy and woe,
So that the ears of Heaven shall deafened be.

[*Passes.*

Voice of VENGEANCE, *descending.*

War, after Discord press more fiercely on.
Whet up thy fangs, and sharpen thy red claws.
Move with the front and seeming of a man,
But with a dragon's heart and ravening maw.
And, to the fierceness of rapacious beasts,
Add cunning of a demon. Cruelty
Shall guide thy steps, Injustice bear thy torch.
Beset this people ; dig a trench about,
And hedge them in on every side. Then feed
Until satiety shall drive thee hence.

Phantom of WAR, *rising.*

Licentiousness shall furnish forth the feast,
And Passions serve it up. I 'll eat, I 'll eat —
Ah ! I 've some appetite. I 'll gorge myself,
And disappear when naught remains to crunch.
[*Passes*

Voice of VENGEANCE, *descending.*

Go, Famine, lead thy latest tortures forth.
Press with thy skinny hand the parching throat
More closely, pinch, and set thy stinging teeth
Deep into quivering vitals ; sharply gripe
Each separate entrail in a thousand parts,
Until each part throb with a thousand pangs.
Tax Nature to the utmost ; yet slay not
At once, but tempt with every loathsome thing
To deep defiling crimes against their laws,
And thus to condemnation press them on.

Phantom of FAMINE, *rising.*

Give ! give ! Oh woe ! Oh woe ! I go ! I go !
I 'll gnaw them to the bone, — I 'll gnaw ! I 'll
  gnaw !
I 'm starving — I am flat with hunger. — Oh !
I 'll drink their slowly wasting blood. Give !
  give !

[*Passes.*

Voice of VENGEANCE, *descending.*

Come, Pestilence, follow thou hard upon
The heels of Famine. Breathe from thy gaunt
  cheeks
Infectious vapors. Let thy rheumy eyes
Distill from their deep hollows poisonous dews.
Shake fevers from thy dank and matted hair,
Where they lie hidden. With thy fingers touch
The centre of each joint, and racking pains
Implant remediless. Burn every nerve,
And fix blaspheming horrors in their souls,
With groans, and wails, and curses tearing
  them.

Phantom of PESTILENCE, *rising.*

All noiseless, swifter than the comet's flight,
Along the setting sun's slant rays, the moon's
Uprising beams, I move; my breath attaints
The air. Aha ! they faint ! I wither them.

[*Passes.*

Voice of VENGEANCE, *descending.*

Thou, Conflagration, be not over fast.
Conceal thy coal-red feet awhile from view
In mists of evening. Gird about thy loins
Thy smoky mantle that it seem a cloud.
Thy head, with its disheveled hair of flame,
Repose upon the setting sun's red couch,
Till Discord, Pestilence, War, Famine, all
Their ills exhaust ; then come thou on with
      Death
Upon thy path, or hidden in thy train,
And leave him naught to do but count his gains.

Phantom of CONFLAGRATION, *rising.*

My chariot is ready, and the winds,
My snorting coursers, prance. I 'll hunt them
      down ;
About them net-like wreathe my lengthening
      arms ;
And gather in my feast. I 'll gloat, I 'll glut.
                                    [*Passes.*

Voice of VENGEANCE, *descending.*

Thou, Desolation, take thy silent seat,
When Discord, War, and Famine from the place,
And Pestilence and Conflagration pass.
There sit alone with thine unmoving eye,
And blackened feet, and moss-grown nether
      limbs,

Their scarred and bony lengths but half con-
  cealed,
And ribbèd sides o'ergrown with deadly vines,
And naked skull, that grins the skeleton
Of soft and beautiful Prosperity,
And let naught human near the accursèd spot.

Phantom of DESOLATION, *rising.*

Ah! I'll be still enough. I will not move,
Nor wink. Serpents shall fawn on me, and
  bats;
And in the dismal hollows of mine ears
The screeching owl, unscared, shall build its nest.
[*Passes.*

A VOICE *from the far heights.*

Amen!
Mercy go.
Weep not for this race,
Doomed to wander through the earth,
Fainting under cross and under scourge,
Expiating sin that reached to heaven,
Till in judgment He shall come
Whom they scourged. Go forth:
Comfort His.
Amen!

TITUS.

Whence these dread forms? Have mine eyes
  played me false?
Roars awful Chaos only in mine ears?

JOSEPHUS.

The Lord hath spoken by His messengers,
And thou hast heard their voice, hast seen their
    shapes.
Go on, nor hesitate, for thou art chosen
The instrument of the Almighty's vengeance.
Into thy hand the city is delivered.

                    [*Exit* TITUS.

Oh woe to thee! alas! beleaguered city.
Oh woe to thee! alas! thou bride of Israel.
Now art thou left alone, alone, O Zion.
Now art thou cursed and fallen, Loved of David.
The Judge of all the earth hath given sentence.
The Judge of all the earth, He hath condemned
    thee.
Swift burn the air His messengers of wrath.
Tremble in silence all ye gazing worlds,
And veil your faces that ye perish not.
Thou Temple of the Mighty King, whose crest
Bears up empyreal glories; from whose heights
Angels alone can gaze, nor fall adown
The unmeasurable space; whose awful steep
Glares dizziness into the wildered brain,
And reverence on the soul; whose dreadful front
No mortal eye can look upon, for rays
Which burn with brightness equal to the sun's;
Within whose walls the Almighty deigned to
    place

His covenant, to meet His chosen people,
Shall we ne'er bow again toward thee to wor-
 ship ?
Must all thine awful grandeur disappear
Like piles magnificent of evening clouds ?
Where shall we worship ?   How address our
 God ?

Enter OFFICER.

OFFICER.

Are they all gone ?   I own I was afraid.

JOSEPHUS.

What hast thou seen ?

OFFICER.

          Such sights as freeze the blood
In warmer veins, and crack the brain apart,
Break the foundations of the judgment up,
And blast the eyes: forms reaching to the clouds,
But through whose ghastly, ribless sides the sun
Looked dully from the west.   Up, up, they came
Like smoke from Hades, only they had voice.
And such a voice ! the thunders of great Jove
Are whispers to it —

JOSEPHUS.

Where wert thou, my man ?

OFFICER.

I dared not go far from thee — I was near —

JOSEPHUS.

Prepare the troop. We must out-run the Eve
To Cæsar's camp.

OFFICER.

I 'll go at once, my Lord.
[*Exit* OFFICER.

JOSEPHUS.

The Lord of terrors speaketh, and the earth
Shakes at His voice. Woe to him who with-
        stands !
Shall man, a worm, dare speak with Thee, O
        Lord ?
Let me adore in silence at Thy feet.

Enter OFFICER.

So soon returned, my friend ? What, is the troop
Afoot ?

OFFICER.

It truly is, my Lord, afoot.
The horses had more wits in their swift heels
Than we in our slow heads, for they had wit
Enough to set their ready wits to work
And run away ; while we 'd but wit enough
To let fright addle the poor wits we had,
Till we were frightened off our feet, and then

Our wits as well were in our heels as heads;
For they were on a level, — useless both.
Ay, verily, my Lord, the troop's afoot
For want of horses. But the camels did
As we, lay still ; and for their wits, like us
They now have addled wits, that's us, to carry.

JOSEPHUS.

Come, let's be gone. Lo ! Titus waits for us.
The air is fresh. 'T will do us good to ride.

A Dungeon.

SEXTUS.

SEXTUS.

If it can be that, in the better world,
Our shades may know each other; if the dead
There conscious live of memory and love,
Some loving prescience shall bid her come
To welcome me upon the heavenly portals.
O joyous hope! O cheering end of doubts!
I am an old man young, and years have grown
Too heavy on me; memory is full
Of disappointments; things not of an hour,
But poising each a life.   O welcome end!
Farewell, ye chill, deriding stars who've mocked
My misery with smiles and quivering lids
Winking your jeers.   Farewell, thou dry-eyed
      moon :
Thy orb looked calmly on.   Could so much woe
Nor move thy showers, nor heave thy tides
      ashore ?
Farewell, thou staring sun, who turned'st not
Thy peering gaze from fate so dark and mourn-
      ful.

8

I leave ye all and go the way to life.
Would I could say farewell to thee, O Titus,
As thou, returned, shalt breathe for me, at
    Rome,
And on the green banks of the Tiber, oft,
With thy dear sighs, a loving last farewell.

Enter SALOME.

SALOME.

O Sextus !

SEXTUS.

        Who art thou ? the place is dim —
That voice — it cannot be ! — turn to the light.

SALOME.

O Sextus !

SEXTUS.

    'T is ! Salome !

SALOME.

        Oh ! at last !

SEXTUS.

Ah speak not, lest I wake and find this too
A dream. Yet speak and let me know I dream
    not.

SALOME.

It is no dream. I will not leave thee more.

SEXTUS.

Salome, is it thee I hold at last?
Or hath the weariness of hope deferred
O'erthrown my reason? Is it mockery
Of a disturbèd fancy? Doth Despair,
To torture, thus deceive me? Art thou real?
I think that thou art real, that it is thou,
Thou, — my Salome. I'm not great enough
To bear the joy which overwhelms me ; no,
Nor can I grasp not e'en the hundredth part
Of ecstasy which presseth on my soul
And holds it still.

SALOME.

O Sextus, feel my heart.
There is but one that beateth thus for thee,
And that's Salome's. Thou wert long in coming.

SEXTUS.

A thousand ages, love. I could not find thee.
I've given the lie direct a million times
To boding, cold Despair — rest here, my life.
Oh for ten thousand powers of consciousness!
So I could feel in each that thou art mine,
And that I hold thee here, here, here, Salome.

SALOME.

But tell me, Sextus —

SEXTUS.

What is it, dear soul?

SALOME.

Perchance I should not ask thee : I would
    know —
It may be that I should not call thee mine.

SEXTUS.

Thine, always thine.

SALOME.

And thou hast never wed?

SEXTUS.

No, never, sweetheart.

SALOME.

Nor hast loved another?

SEXTUS.

Oh never once, my life.

SALOME.

I am so fond;
I who should be so humble am so jealous.
Oh I have loved thee so.

SEXTUS.

Who hath loved thee
Could never love another; thee I loved,
And loving once loved always. Think it not
A faithful constancy of love in me,
But constant power of loveliness in thee,
Whose memory hath been to me a shrine
Where all my heart's devotion, satisfied,
Hath bowed, and never sought another temple.

SALOME.

And hast thou truly loved me all these years?
I 'm so unworthy of such love, I think
It cannot be, save when thou tell'st me so.
So tell me still, so make me still believe.
Oh this is love, outlasting wrongs, neglect,
The blights of absence, frosts of hopelessness.
I knew that thou wert living, for Fame told
Thy noble deeds e'en in the forest coverts,
And Hope could cherish fires of constant love.
But thou didst think me dead, or lost for aye —

SEXTUS.

Yet felt that thy loved spirit could not die,
To that was wedded, nor would be divorced.
And so I 've loved but thee.

SALOME.

Oh how my voyage

Across life's sea hath dreary been and void.
What bring I to the haven but full regrets?
A bark so freighted, with such love and hopes,
To be so turned from the desired port,
As was mine own by mine own wicked act,
And driven, torn by currents, adverse winds,
Its precious freight in the first gale thrown o'er,
To find the haven but now when worn and
     wrecked,
When night is falling, driven by a tempest.

SEXTUS.

It is not night for us, my love. My breast
Shall be thy haven; 't is but mid-afternoon.
Our sun is breaking from the clouds at length.
While holding thee, Hope brightens all the future.
And when our evening comes, together we,
Still lovers, in the calm and peaceful twilight,
Still pledging our fond love, will go to rest.

SALOME.

Oh that I never, never had fled from thee!
Ah! I have dreamed such loving things for thee
That I would do; have felt my heart so full
Of tenderness, of sympathy and love,
All cherished as a hoarded treasure for thee;
Have yearned so to requite thee for thy wrongs,
That all of life hath seemed to me too short

For what love would have done for thee and me.
I would have planted roses which should spring
Beneath thy feet, and made thee a sweet bed
Of sweet forget-me-nots and violets;
Ta'en off thine armor when thou wert aweary,
And wakened thee with songs, thy slumbers
    o'er.
But now the journey 's finished, and, alas!
I have done naught for thee but make thee
    mourn.
A cloud upon thy day, and, in thy night,
A haunting sadness — Ah! I know it, Sextus.

SEXTUS.

But these dear moments, which they make the
    dearer,
Repay the sorrows of a weary life
Of waiting, fading hopes. Thou lovest me,
Hast ever loved me —

SALOME.

    Always, always, Sextus.

SEXTUS.

And now —

SALOME.

    We will no more be parted, love.
But tell me —

SEXTUS.

Tell thee what? How pale thou art!
And worn and wasted! My poor, suffering child.

SALOME.

How wast thou made a prisoner? By whom?

SEXTUS.

I was with Titus at Antonia
Reviewing all the siege, when, suddenly,
I heard a mocking voice calling my name,
And taunting me with loss of thee in Britain.
It was Kaliphilus—

SALOME.

Kaliphilus!
And here!

SEXTUS.

He was within the city, and I leaped,
Possessed but by one thought and wish for
    vengeance,
Alone into the throng of armèd Jews,
And through them, yielding, sought my mock-
    ing foe,
Who, still retreating, drew me from the wall,
Until, assailed upon the bloody pavement
By the returning Jews under his guidance,
I slipped and fell. Thus overthrown, their blows

Fell like a shower of stones upon me while
Defending still myself, as best I could,
And slaying many of them, till, at length,
My helmet was displaced, a well aimed blow
Drove Consciousness from its accustomed seat,
And, when it had its rightful throne regained,
I was a prisoner; Kaliphilus
My master. Presently some soldiers came
And brought me to this dungeon. Scarce two
    hours
Have taken their dread record from the earth
Since I was placed here.

SALOME.

           By Kaliphilus!
Oh doth he haunt us still? I thought him
    hence.

SEXTUS.

How didst thou find me, love? Or art thou
    here,
By fierce compulsion of some enemy,
A prisoner, like me?

SALOME.

          Compelled by love,
I came to thee most willingly. Just now
Was proclamation by a herald made
That thou wert prisoned in the Castle, and—

SEXTUS.

And that at dawn I should be crucified.
But be not troubled. Titus will not sleep
Until he shall take vengeance, for he loves me.
And now, since I have thee and fain would live,
Hope tells me that, ere morn, we shall be free.
So let us think but of the happiness
Of these dear moments, each well worth a life.

SALOME.

Oh I am happy, Sextus, oh! so blessed
In feeling thy dear arms again about me,
And once more resting here my weary head,
Which hath found rest upon no other pillow.
But dost thou know — how could'st thou — hast
        thou heard
That I 'm a Christian?

SEXTUS.

Yea, I know it, love.

SALOME.

And lovest me no less?

SEXTUS.

                No less, my own.
And art thou now most happy? Is there naught
Could add unto thy bliss?

SALOME.

But one thing, love.

SEXTUS.

And that is?

SALOME.

Could I know that thou, too, art
A Christian.

SEXTUS.

Then be blest, for so I am.

SALOME.

Thou art! thou art? The Lord in heaven
  be praised.
How can I thank thee, Saviour merciful?
Accept the feeble wishes of my heart
To offer Thee some better service. Now
No harm can any more come to us. God,
The Lord of Israel, 's a mighty tower
Which cannot be removed; a city walled
In which the righteous dwell in safety. God,
The Lord of Israel, 's a strong defense;
With shield of mercy, sword of flaming wrath,
He guardeth tenderly His children. God,
The Lord of Israel, will not forget,
And none may blind Him that He cannot see,
Nor stop His ears; He sleepeth never. God,
The Lord of Israel, will try His saints,

Yet cometh in their dire extremity
To manifest His constant love and power.
But tell me, how thou didst become a Christian.

SEXTUS.

I will betimes ; but first recount to me
Thy story since that dreadful day in Britain.
Canst thou forgive me?   I so wronged thee
        there.

SALOME.

Forgive thee, Sextus ?   Fie ! the only wrong
Thou ever didst me was to ask me this.

SEXTUS.

Oh that I could enfold thee in my being,
Soul of my soul, and heart within my heart.
Where hast thou been ?   Why could I find
        thee not?

SALOME.

Kaliphilus bore me aboard his ship,
Where Thona and Bernice were already,
At once set sail, but, ere we reached a haven,
We, by a storm, were driven on the coast
Of Germany, made captive by the Germans,
All save Kaliphilus, who, cursing, fled
With cries and groans, as if tormenting fiends
Were driving him.   His slave, an ugly thing,
Was by them slain.

SEXTUS.

May furies hunt him ever!

SALOME.

O Sextus, be not unforgiving.

SEXTUS.

What?

Canst thou forgive him?

SALOME.

Yea, I hope so, love.
Our captors brought us straightway to their
 chief,
Who, smitten with distemper, helpless lay.
Benignant Mercy, at our intercession,
Restored him to his people strong in health.
Then were we held as envoys of their gods,
And kept so sacredly that no escape
Was open for us. Once, when Lepidus
Had almost rescued us, by chance they learned
His purpose, bore us to their sacred grove,
In depths of forests inaccessible,
And guarded us from all approach, save that
Of their own chief and priests and loving
 people.

SEXTUS.

Friend Lepidus brought me thy letter, sweet,

And that first made me wish to know the
    Christ.
I sought out Paul, a mighty preacher, then
In Rome. who kindly led me to His feet.
And Lepidus informed me how he found
And lost you in the wilds. How came you
    thence ?

SALOME.

'T was after many months, when wars had
    drawn
The tribe upon our borders, that, one day
When warriors and women all had gone
On a foray into a Roman province,
Save some infirm old priests, we took our way
Unto the nearest Roman fortress. Long
And wearisome our march, guided alone
By stars at night, and hidden in the day.
We reached, at length, an outpost. There we
    learned
That, with Vespasian in Palestine,
Thou, and good Lepidus, wert in the field
Against the warring Jews. But one wish, then,
Possessed my soul, — to see Jerusalem
Once more, and find thee here.

SEXTUS.

My faithful love.

SALOME.

As best we could we made the journey thence
To Rome. Nor there we tarried, for a company
Of forces gave us escort strong to Tyre,
And thence we came unto Jerusalem,
Where we were told the army soon would be.
I went to kneel before the sepulchres
Of Christ and John the Baptist; and, with tears
And many prayers and fastings, sought anew
Forgiveness, and fresh zeal, and greater love.
Soon I fell ill, and, ere sweet Health upreared
My prostrate form and led me from my couch,
The gates were closed. Sedition held misrule,
The Roman walls encompassed all the city,
Egress was none, nor safety anywhere.

SEXTUS.

Oh my poor, wearied dove, hast thou at length
Found this poor ark? But it shall shelter thee
Until the floods o'erwhelm it, or the storms
Drive it to wreck. How thou hast suffered,
     love.
If we escape the dangers of this night,
As let us hope we shall, all will be well.

SALOME.

Ah! it is fatal! I shall not go hence.
His will be done.

SEXTUS.

What words are these? What fears?
What see'st thou, love? Why dost thou gaze
    about
As if thine eyes would pierce the flinty walls?

SALOME.

This is the dungeon where John Baptist died.
I knew it not till now. Oh 't is decreed!
My crime looks frowningly upon me.

SEXTUS.

    Hush!
Lift now thine eyes to heaven in faith and see
The merciful Redeemer smiles on thee.

SALOME.

Oh let Thy mercy pardon me that crime;
Oh cleanse me, Saviour, Thou All-Pitying.
'T was such a night — so many years ago —
And I am hither led — but not by Chance.
Though Justice oft comes slowly, yet she
    comes —

SEXTUS.

Away these sad forebodings! Let 's rejoice
That we are met; and that we here are met.
Let it be sign of peace and joy to thee,
A proof of thine acquittal. Cheer thee, love.

Enter a GUARD.

GUARD.

Come forth, Salome. Thou art ordered forth.

SALOME.

What! now? So soon? I cannot leave thee —
stay.
Oh kiss me, Sextus, — we shall surely meet.
Not long can we be separated now.

SEXTUS.

Ah! will they tear thee from me? Still a kiss,
My bliss on earth, and guide to heavenly bliss.

SALOME.

The Father's peace, passing all understanding;
The Son's great love, redeeming from all error;
The Spirit's comfort, healing every sorrow,
Be with, redeem, and comfort thee forever.

9

A Chamber in the Castle.

KALIPHILUS.

KALIPHILUS.

WILL she flee from me now, as others do,
Though I approach not nor attempt to woo?
Ah! will she curse me? Shall I now be left
Of this sole hope, my comfort sole, bereft?

Enter GUARD, *with* SALOME.

[*Exit* GUARD

SALOME.

Kaliphilus!

KALIPHILUS.

Nay, do not fly — 't is vain.
Yet tremble not. I will not harm thee — stay.
To none but thee can I my woes unfold.
What! Thou dost fear me too, and dread, and
hate?
All creatures do, and, as the ages roll
Shall they more fear, and hold me more in awe,
Till I shall fly them. No way can I turn
And feel one warming ray of sympathy.

SALOME.

What can I do for thee?

KALIPHILUS.

          Oh, thou canst ease
My agony. Let me but talk to thee,
Look on thee, hear thee speak, and know thy
    heart
Doth not abhor me.

SALOME.

          Ah! I pity thee.
Thou knowest it already, and I pray —

KALIPHILUS.

Pray? pray! to whom? for what? for me?
    Oh fie!
Pray not for me.

SALOME.

       Then can I naught for thee.

KALIPHILUS.

I have so suffered! I must suffer so!
Unnumbered ages from the future roll,
Each moment of each age an endless hell;
Each moment of the past an endless hell.
For lo! I stand within my memory,
As in a prison-house of heated bronze,
Whose pictured walls, in red-hot characters,
Look on me, live, speak, move, and tear my
    soul.

132

Turn now thy thoughts to heavenly things, and
then —

KALIPHILUS.

See how they throng! I cannot name them.
All
Are clutching at me, and in vain I flee.
For every crime and meanness of my life
Hath there a visage dread, or mocking grin,
And arms, like mists, to reach infinity,
And hands of heated steel which snatch my
soul,
And drag apart my brain, and rend my heart.
But, dreadfullest of all, the Eye that burns
In black, impenetrable Darkness, which
At all times moves before me, and from whence
A voice, which never speaks, forever says:
Bear on thy burden till I come again.

SALOME.

But bear it penitently and with patience —

KALIPHILUS.

And so to live forever, adding still
Each hour some devil crime, some haunting
thought,
Some serpent secret at my heart to gnaw,

And wreathe its deadly coils about my brain,
To those which torture now.

SALOME.

What shall I do?
How help thee? Why complain to —

KALIPHILUS.

Why complain?
Why do I humble thus myself to thee
As I will not before Omnipotence?
Because I love thee —

SALOME.

Pray thee, let me go —

KALIPHILUS.

Because when thee I lose, I then must bear
In silence evermore my agonies,
Nor pity find, nor listening sympathy,
Affection none, nor aught but awe and dread.
I will not harm thee, nay, I dare not do it.
Should aught but reverent love for thee awake
In me, 't would rouse ten thousand fiends to tear
And hunt me hence. So was I driven from
      thee,
When, cast upon the shores of Germany,
I fled and left thee unprotected there.

SALOME.

But I was cared for by Almighty Love.

KALIPHILUS.

And I was scourged by merciless tormentors.
I wandered through the savage wilds of Eu-
rope,
Through northern realms of Asia, where the
snows,
On down-bent branches resting of low trees,
Make them appear the tents of Winter's hosts
Encamped, and waiting for the signal trump
Of storms, reposing, which shall lead them
south
To ravage and to reign. And there I hoped,
By frosts congealed, to grow insensible,
And feel no more my doom. A lying hope!
Nor cold congeals, nor heat can melt my flesh.
I swore to end myself, defied my Judge —

SALOME.

Oh spare me, I would hear no more, unless
Thou dost repent, and this is thy confession —

KALIPHILUS.

And, walking still, I reached the Eastern bound
Of the broad continent, where yet no foot,
Save that of savage beast, or man more savage,

Had ever trod. But there I stayed not. On
Into the sea I fain would go, that there
Its raging waves or monsters should destroy me.
But all in vain. I walked the waters as
I had the mountains and the vales of snow,
Till, cursing the Omnipotence which held
Me thus a miracle upon the surge,
And plunging madly on the unopening waves
To force an ingress, shrieking blasphemies,
And hurling fierce defiance at His Throne,
Upon a sudden fell a lightning bolt,
Which opened under me a yawning gulf,
And to the ocean's farthest depths I sank.
The waters over me joined with a roar
As of a thousand thunders met in battle,
And shut me from the hated light of heaven.

SALOME.

Dost thou invent a tale?

KALIPHILUS.

Nay, in good sooth.
Still could I see, still hear, and on the dark
And oozy bottom of the ocean walk
As on dry land. No swimming fish e'er
    breathed
The watery element more free than I.
A murmur strikes upon my startled ear,

Increasing ever, growing terrible,
Surrounding me, and coming ever nearer.
And now I see the monsters of the deep
Approaching. From each side all living things
Which swim the flood, crawl from its poison-
    ous slime,
In its dark caverns lurk, or lie in wait
Behind its weedy crags, in horrid phalanx
Come round and over me, and roar, and hiss,
And shriek: with fins, and claws, and out-
    stretched tongues,
And long arms point at me, and still the noise
More hideous grows, and seems to scream the
    words,
Go faster, Jew; go faster. Vainly now
Would I mount up and reach the solid earth.
I could not rise. The waters over me
Pressed like the world on fabled Atlas' shoul-
    ders.

SALOME.

And didst thou then repent?

KALIPHILUS.

                I scorned the thought.
Upon the bottom still I walked, and walked,
In agony unspeakable, while dread
And loathing, deathly pains, and awe
Convulsed me. Still they drove me on, nor
    ceased

To point at me, and leer, and lash, and sting,
And shriek, and hiss, and roar in hideous chorus,
Go faster, Jew ; go faster.   On, still on,
Through fearful valleys, over caverned hills,
By shuddering sea-groves whence new horrors
    crawled,
Each, all, from every side, joining the hunt,
I passed, nor rested, nor could rest, nor stop,
A time which seemed ten centuries of woe.
At last I climbed a long and steep ascent,
The light grew greener, paler, brighter, and
The watery fiends began to disappear.
Then, presently, I mounted to the air,
And stood alone on land, where from my feet
The ocean westward rolled, and, going down,
The Sun upon a watery bed reposed.

SALOME.

Where wert thou ?   In what land ?

KALIPHILUS.

             That knew I not.
Had I been driven darkling through the deep
Around the Earth's remotest southern cape
To stand again on Europe's western shore ?
It could not be, for I had wandered o'er
That coast from north to south, and naught
    was here

E'er seen by me before. The sun's slant rays
A myriad of tiny stars received
Set in the firmament of purest snow,
Which covered all the land. I southward
 turned,
And wandered on in haste still southward,
 southward,
Through climes which ever grew more genial,
Until in tropic heats I stood. The Sun
Above me drove his glowing course athwart
The zenith. All around me strange flowers
 bloomed,
Such as, in Paradise, our parents saw.
And birds, which looked like flying flowers,
 rejoiced
In every tone of music. Beasts, unseen
Till then by me, there reveled in wild life,
But left their prey, their quarrels, and their
 sports
To join in one discordant chorus, howling,
As me they chased, *Go faster, Jew; go faster.*
The reptiles hissed and roared, *Go faster, Jew.*
The birds, from dark clouds, screamed, *Go
 faster, Jew.*
On, on I went, the Sun his daily course
To northward guiding more and more each day,
And temperate warmth succeeded tropic heats.
By cloud-capped mountains, through vast plains
 , and meadows,

Across deep rivers, whose wide floods appeared
Like broad and endless lakes, in which the tides
Flowed but one way in never ceasing currents,
I passed, till Frost o'er snows and realms of ice
Held constant sway, and breathed on all his cold.
And now the sun drove swiftly through the
    north.
I back returned to where I first set foot
Upon this new world; thence, across the main,
To shores of Asia and the old world came.
Whence, through more southern climes, to
    Germany
I went in search of thee —

SALOME.

                Forget, I beg —

KALIPHILUS.

I sooner could forget my doom than thee
Who caused it. Thence I traced thee slowly
    hither.
When death shall summon thee beyond my
    reach
To that new world will I return, and bear,
As Jupiter Europa o'er the sea —
The story is by Grecian poets told —
Some fair companion, and these wilds shall be
Peopled by us with wanderers like me.
Oh I'll beget a cursed and rebel race —

SALOME.

Oh, let me go. I pray thee, let me go.

KALIPHILUS.

Salome, for this hour I've waited years.
Be not unkind. The only rest I hope
Until, in judgment, He shall come again,
Is talking thus with thee. Come to this window.
Behold these wretches fly the boon I crave.

CHORUS *without; PRIESTS, in sackcloth passing.*

Help, Lord.
The storms increase!
Will anger never cease?
Deals Justice now the stern award?
Out of the depths, O Lord, we call.
The billows over us!
They cover us!
We fall!

[*Exeunt* PRIESTS.

Enter JEWS, *flying.*

CHORUS *without,* JEWS.

Pursued! pursued of God!
Ah! No escape!
At His almighty nod
.Lo! wrath, in fiery shape,
From His pavilion dark
Rides forth and shakes the ground

By its dread going, — hark !
With hiss and swoop and thunder sound
It cometh! fly! Oh fly!
Red vengeance rushes on us from the sky !

[*Exeunt* JEWS, *flying.*

SALOME.

Is this a time to woo and tell me tales
When thou couldst aid thy wretched country-
men ?

KALIPHILUS.

Aid but by killing, curse by guarding life.
They know not what they fear, nor what they
wish.
The Almighty surely laughs to see the fools
So blindly fleeing sure relief from torture.
Now is their fear, now their calamity.
Is this a time to woo ? I tell thee, woman,
All times to me are like. Now must I woo
While I can make thee listen to me. When
Thou shalt have passed unto the realms of rest,
Naught shall remain for me, until He come,
But to be great as was my daring, ay,
And like a devil bear my punishment,
Meet for a devil, walking to and fro,
And up and down the earth in haught en-
durance.
The agony that breaks and crushes me
Down like an Ætna, wrath of the Infinite,

Shall find no voice, nor shall I more complain,
But vent my anguish in great deeds of spite ;
Desiring all things, friendship, enmity,
Love without awe, and hatred without dread,
Ay, parents, brothers, sisters, children, youth,
The sweet and natural coming on of age,
And wounds, and sickness unto death, death,
      death, —
All, any thing which might make me a man
Like others among men, and all in vain.

SALOME.

Thou may'st be loved ; do good, be kind and
    true.

KALIPHILUS.

The dupe of many, the desire of few.

SALOME.

Let Conscience tell thee that thou hast done
    well.

KALIPHILUS.

I care not what the bigot Conscience tell.

SALOME.

Instead of ill, plot good, if plot thou will.

KALIPHILUS.

'T is His decree that evil I plot still.

I am accursed all, save my love for thee,
Which is divine, so from the curse is free.
When once that love is taken from my heart,
I shall be cursed and devilish every part.

SALOME.

But I have prayed for thee, shall pray for thee.
Bernice, too —

KALIPHILUS.

Bernice !

SALOME.

Thou 'st not asked
For her.

KALIPHILUS.

I loved her once. Oh, she was fair,
When in her native valley I beheld her, —
The fairest blooming flower of womanhood.

SALOME.

But she is dead.

KALIPHILUS.

I know it.

SALOME.

Died to-day.

KALIPHILUS.

I know it.

SALOME.

In the city here.

KALIPHILUS.

I know it.

SALOME.

She bade me say that she had ever loved thee.

KALIPHILUS.

Tell me not of it. What! will thou smite too?
Is she not with the rest pursuing me?

SALOME.

Since I can naught for thee, oh send me hence.

KALIPHILUS.

But thou canst aught for me. Give me one kiss.
Oh, shrink not from this prayer. Give me one
    kiss.

SALOME.

A kiss of charity thou askest not:
A kiss of love to thee I cannot give.

KALIPHILUS.

What! Shall I take it? Know that thou art
    mine,
A prisoner.

SALOME.

And hast thou dared to woo
And talk of love to one thou hast beguiled —

KALIPHILUS.

Nay, come, forget that, by his subtlety,
Love brought thee here to throne thee in my
life.
This rule queen absolute, as Rome the world.
Be not Mount Zion, beauty of the earth,
Obdurate, trembling in the arms of force.

SALOME.

Cease, cease, thy words are vain. I hear thee
not.

KALIPHILUS.

But thou must hear, Salome ; I must speak.
The dignity of man's true love compels
A hearing. Brief my speech. I coin no words
To jingle sweetly. Baby loves may choose
A wordy effervescence ; I will pour
The unstirred liquor, clear and deep and strong.
I love thee —

SALOME.

If thou lov'st me let me go.
So shalt thou prove thy love.

KALIPHILUS.

Thou shalt not go.
With me is Love no coward. Men for love
Dare death. My love dares greater things and
worse.

10

SALOME.

Approach me not lest pity turn to scorn.

KALIPHILUS.

The oil of that sharp scorn feedeth the fire
Which heateth me, and setteth it to flame.
Ah! I will have thee, thy disdain, thy pride;
For thou shalt be all mine, yea, every sigh
I 'll seize escaping from thy parted lips
As would a conqueror escaping men
From citadels on fire. Cold as thou art
With haughtiness, I 'll make thee glow with
        love,
And sigh, and weep; for tears shall from thee
        fall
As showers, for very heat, in summer; yea,
I 'll woo, I 'll swear, I 'll promise like a lover.
Thou shalt be mistress, queen, ay, empress,
        more,
Most difficult of all, thou shalt rule me,
Kaliphilus unconquered. I will know
No difference betwixt thy flesh and mine,
Save that thine own 's immeasurably dearer.
Yea, saw I Hades in thy dark eye's depths,
And waves of fire where glow thy haughty lips,
I would embrace thee. But thine eye is heaven,
Thy mouth a fount of nectar. Yield thee,
        yield.

SALOME.

If thou art man, thou wilt no more offend
My sense with words unseemly; if thou art
    brute,
Thy words are roarings, made but to express
The rage of passion. Talkest thou of love ?
Thou hast no symptom of that sweet disease.
Thou canst not know it for thou dost not feel it:
It is the malady of noble natures.

KALIPHILUS.

Old Antony, to win his cup of love,
Dissolved an empire in 't, and drank it down,
And felt more life glow through his swelling
    veins
In one swift moment of that thrilling draught
Than in a thousand years of kingly rule.
I would outdo him, for my love is greater.
I go not hence without thee. Pray thee, yield.

SALOME.

I will not.

KALIPHILUS.

    If thou stay, thou here shalt perish,
For Simon holds thee on the capital charge
That thou art Christian.

SALOME.

    This by thy contriving.

KALIPHILUS.

Be mine, I 'll save thee ; and, for thy dear sake
I will save Sextus —

SALOME

I will ne'er be thine.
Avaunt! fell schemer. 'T is thine ancient snare.
To save my Sextus' life I did such wrong
As Heaven weeps at; hence come all my woes.
To save my father's life again did wrong.
I can do so no more. God's will be done.

KALIPHILUS.

If thou yield not, then take I thee by force.

SALOME.

Lift not thine hand upon me. For the Lord
Omnipotent, in mercy infinite,
Is infinite in wrath. Look to thyself.
He will protect all those that trust in Him.
Thy words are daring ; let thy words suffice.
Thou durst not, by thine acts, profane His
    image.
Thou durst not, by thine acts, defy my trust
In Him. He 's ever near me. Fear His ven-
    geance.
Shrink back in shame that thou would'st un-
    dertake

An act of meanness which the devils would
scorn.
Ay, to thy knees —

KALIPHILUS.

To pray thee pardon me —

SALOME.

And ask His pardon whom thou would'st offend.

KALIPHILUS.

Her power of virtue awes my daring soul.
Yet will I have, subject her, and control.

Enter Simon and attendants.

SIMON.

Behold! a dread portent is in the sky!
In middle heavens a blazing sword is hung
Above the city, lengthening ever down.
Like a whole world in conflagration burns,
Over the Temple in the western sky,
A comet, and its flames, athwart the pole,
In lurid brightness stream. Stars fall in show-
ers,
Although the blood-red sun be not yet set,
As if the Almighty's breath, a raging storm,
Shook them mature from their empyreal stems.
O come, behold it. Tell us what it means.

150 SALOME.

KALIPHILUS.

Return her to the dungeon ; guard her well.

[SALOME *is led out.*

I 'll go with thee, and what I can will tell.

A Dungeon.

SEXTUS *and* SALOME.

SALOME.

KALIPHILUS hath ta'en us in his net.

SEXTUS.

But Titus surely shall undo his cunning.

SALOME.

Let's trust in Him who only can redeem.

SEXTUS.

Oh could I see the lances of my legion!

SALOME.

Let thoughts of vengeance enter not thy soul.

SEXTUS.

When hither brought a prisoner, I repined
That so my life must end, which should have
    failed
Or in the battle-field, or in thine arms;

Yet had, with sweet contentment, welcomed
    death.
But since thou camest to me, as the angel
Deliverer to the Apostle came,
The chains Despondency had wrought upon
My limbs have fallen ; what was dark is light.
I doubly am content to live, and Hope
Spreads her bright wings and buoys my spirit
    up —

Enter THONA.

THONA.

The guards permit, oh let me stay with thee.

SALOME.

Rash children! have ye come to die with me?

Enter CHORUS, *Christians.*

CHORUS.

Behold!
In arms of gold
Squadrons and hosts of soldiers move
Upon embankèd clouds above
The western sun ;
And chariots run
To battle in the sky ;
And conquered myriads fly
From flaming cities falling ;
About them clouds with blood grow red,

Like a well foughten field
Where hosts on hosts are fiercely led,
The lookers-on appalling.
And engines wield
The huge artillery of war,
And smite the crumbling towers from far.
The people mute with terror stand,
The useless brand falls from the nerveless
  hand.

Enter MARAH.

MARAH.

Why stay ye here? The guards with fear are
  faint,
And, to behold portents upon the clouds,
Have left their posts unguarded. Up! away!
What, know ye not, ye both in the same snare
Are taken, and are held for present death?
Kaliphilus with Simon hath conspired
Against your heads. By seeming to accede,
As an accomplice in their wicked plot,
I know of what I speak. Fly, fly at once.
The way is open. Seek your hiding place.
Delay not. Look that ye shall leave no trace
For their blood-hounds to follow. Once more
  free,
For succor and for safety trust to me.

SALOME.

O Sextus, fly, and Thona shall conduct thee,
Under God's guidance, to a place of safety.
Once there, consult ye further. I will stay,
And thus, perchance, their hot pursuit delay.

SEXTUS.

Nay, thou shalt not —

SALOME.

Be governed now by me,
And thou shalt free me when thou shalt be
free.

MARAH.

'T is better thus, would ye the current stem
Of rolling dangers —

SEXTUS.

Dear love, go with them.

MARAH.

Why wilt thou linger ? Men for reason slow,
For swift wit women. Haste thee, let us go.

SEXTUS.

Come thou, Salome, I will find a sword —

MARAH.

One sword, e'en thine, against this raging
    horde!
'T is mine to care for her. Nay, leave her,
    come.

SEXTUS.

What! leave thee, child? What, leave thee,
    my own love?
What! I, a man, a soldier, leave my love
Here in this den of wolves to escape myself?
It cannot be. Go thou, or I go not.

SALOME.

Nay, Sextus, trust to Marah. Her sharp wit
Shall like a sharp tooth gnaw the hunter's net
And set the lion free; and, when thou art free,
Then use thy manly strength and soldier's skill
To free me also. So shall both be saved.
It is my wish. O Sextus, I entreat —

SEXTUS.

What shall I do?

MARAH.

        Haste, ere the guards return.

SEXTUS.

So leave thee, so desert —

SALOME.

So rescue me.

SEXTUS.

Love hath so riveted mine arms about thee
I cannot let thee go.

MARAH

Art thou a Roman ?
Thy women would upbraid and cry thee shame.

SALOME.

Go, Sextus, go ; soon shall we meet again.
It is thy duty, Sextus.

SEXTUS.

One more kiss.
I go because thou will'st it — still a kiss,
And if it be the last one —

MARAH.

Haste thee, haste.

SEXTUS.

Farewell, Salome.   Oh, I am ashamed
To leave thee thus.   Be of good courage, love.

SALOME.

God bless thee, Sextus; now thou lovest me.

SEXTUS.

I go, my own love, but to rescue thee.

SALOME.

Go, all, my children ; tarry not, but fly.

[*Exeunt* SEXTUS, MARAH, THONA, *and* CHORUS.

It may suffice for all if I should die.

A Hall in the Castle.

SIMON.

BRING here the prisoners.

[*Exeunt* FIRST OFFICER *and some* GUARDS.

We 'll question them ;
Arraign Salome on the capital charge
That she is Roman, and hath been concealed,
The spy of Titus and confederate,
Within the city ; then, with show of mercy,
Entice from her all knowledge, which she owns,
Of Roman dispositions and affairs ;
And when she shall have won the promised
    grace
By so accepting our so proffered terms,
Betraying to us all her master's plans,
Shall it be proven that she is a Christian,
And hostile to our state and our religion,
A plotter for the nation's overthrow,
And, for these practices, shall be condemned,
And with her Sextus, to be crucified.

Enter FIRST OFFICER *and* GUARDS, *with* SALOME.

But where is Sextus ?

FIRST OFFICER.

Sextus hath escaped.

SIMON.

Escaped!

FIRST OFFICER.

Escaped, my Lord.

SIMON.

Go, take his guards,
And cast them headlong to the Romans.   Halt!
See that thou take them to the highest tower
And cast them thence.

FIRST OFFICER.

My Lord, it shall be done.
[*Exeunt* FIRST OFFICER *and some* GUARDS.

SIMON.

Call out thy men, and search the city through,
Discover Sextus, or see me no more.
[*Exit* SECOND OFFICER.

Salome, it is known thou art a Roman,
And that thou hast within the city been
Concealed, the spy of our detested foes,
The spring of their obduracy and spite.

SALOME.

'T is true, I have within the city dwelt,

Constrained, like others, by the unyielding siege,
Yet peacefully; nor with affairs of state
Nor war's great questions have I mingled, but,
As best I could, have succored the distressed.

SIMON.

The mercy shown to Hebrews who escape,
And flee unto the Romans, should we show.
Look from the wall, behold on every tree
A Jewish body crucified.   The vales
Are pestilent with odors from the corpses
Of Jews ripped up that Roman soldiers in them
Might seek for plunder; and the air is full
Of sighs, and groans, and supplications, cries
Of agony, and sounds of swinging scourges.

SALOME.

I know the scene is dreadful, yea, I know it.
Ah! would that I could stay such cruel deeds!
But I can only pray that wars may cease.

SIMON.

That thou art Roman is thy condemnation.
The more since it appears that thou didst aid
The prisoner Sextus to escape —

SALOME.

                                        Alas!
I could not aid him.

SIMON.

Knowest thou who did?
Why answerest thou not? Speak out.

SALOME.

I know.

SIMON.

And whither he hath fled?

SALOME.

How could I know
Since I went not with him?

SIMON.

Question thou not.
And wert thou privy to his purpose? Speak,
Knew'st thou where he would go?

SALOME.

I heard them say.

SIMON.

Then tell us quickly.

SALOME.

Nay. I may not tell.

11

SIMON.

Know'st thou the names of those who helped
    him hence?

SALOME.

I know them.

SIMON.

What are they?

SALOME.

I may not tell.

SIMON.

Beware! beware! Now makest thou thyself
Confederate with them. Look thou, Salome,
It is our purpose to deal gently with thee.
Although the charge, that thou art Roman here,
Now stands confessed, it shall not work thee
    harm
If thou wilt but inform us what thou knowest
Of Sextus, and of those who took him hence,
And of the plans and forces of the Romans.

SALOME.

The plans and forces of the Romans are
To me unknown. I came not here to war,
Nor to engage in stratagems and wiles.

SIMON.

But thou canst tell us of the plot to rescue

Our prisoner; who was the chief contriver,
And who the assistants. So shalt thou escape
The penalty due to thy presence here.

SALOME.

I would not so escape.

SIMON.

Dost thou refuse ?

SALOME.

I do.

SIMON.

Think well. For now these many years
The Romans are our masters and instructors.
And they have taught us all the arts of tor-
    ment.
Its bloody characters are writ upon
Our bodies till we are its library,
And ne'er magician had so dreadful books.
Now, like ambitious youths just from the school,
We burn for fit occasion to employ
The skill we 've learned upon our skillful
    teachers.
We thirst to be revenged, in kind, upon
The Romans. Be not thou the victim first
Who shall encounter all this raging thirst.

SALOME.

I cannot tell thee aught that thou would'st
know.

SIMON.

Yea, thou canst tell us whither Sextus fled.

SALOME.

I may not.

SIMON.

May not? May not? Wilt not.

SALOME.

Will not.

SIMON.

Then shall thine obstinacy cost thee dear.
Thou art a Christian : canst thou this deny?

SALOME.

I am a Christian.

SIMON.

By thine impious acts
The city is accursed, and shall be ruined,
Unless a punishment, meet for thy crimes,
Be brought upon thee; or a sacrifice
Be made atonement for thy forfeit life.
If thou shalt guide our search to Sextus, and
The traitors who have rescued him, thy life

Shall be redeemed by theirs, and thou shalt go
In freedom to the Romans. Wilt thou so ?

SALOME.

I will not. Naught that human power may do
Can save this city. Know that it must fall ;
But not by acts of Christians. Their great Head
Pronounced its doom for manifold transgres-
    sions,
And when ye see it come to pass, believe.

SIMON.

Thou hast condemned thyself; for ye, to prove
Prophetic power of that Impostor now
Would cause fulfillment of His prophecy,
E'en by destruction of this holy city.
But thou shalt not escape due punishment,
Yet shalt discovery make of that vile treason
Which lurketh in our midst, and hath pre-
    vailed
To snatch this Sextus from the grasp of ven-
    geance.
But Vengeance hath long arms and many hands,
And many ears, and many eyes that sleep not.
Return, and in thy dungeon see prepared
The torture which shall draw thy secrets out.
Ay, thou shalt cry those secrets out so loud,
The Roman camp shall hear itself betrayed.

And, that no point of anguish be o'erlooked,
I will, myself, be executioner,
And I will question thee upon the rack.
I have a fecund and a ready wit
Which shall not fail, though ne'er so strongly
    locked,
To ope the doors of that defiant castle
Where thou dost guard thy hidden, guilty
    knowledge.

CHORUS *without*, Jews.

Woe! woe! Alas!
Alas! We are undone!
The sacrifice hath failed!
The daily sacrifice is ended!
The blood of priests and foemen blended!
The holiest place assailed!
Lo! Vengeance is begun!
Woe! woe! Alas!

Woe! woe! Alas!
Howl Kedron, Olivet.
Storms raise your wailing voices high,
O Earthquakes, rend the garment of the earth.
O Mountains, give your burning torrents birth.
Winds, shriek forth woes, and shrieking fly;
For Mercy's sun is set.
Woe! woe! Alas!

Enter FIRST OFFICER.

SIMON.

What means this new outcry?

FIRST OFFICER.

The sacrifice,
The daily sacrifice, hath failed. In terror
The people rend their garments and bewail.

SIMON.

Why hath it failed?

FIRST OFFICER.

Since John hath held the Temple,
He with his zealots, as thou knowest well,
Hath driven thence the priests, all sacrilege
Hath compassed, till no men remain to make
The offering —

Enter SECOND OFFICER.

SIMON.

And what news bringest thou?

SECOND OFFICER.

A herald from the Roman camp demands
A parley with thee.

SIMON.

We will see him straight.

Return the prisoner to the dungeon ; there
Make ready torments; guard her till I come.

[*Exeunt* OFFICER *and* GUARDS, *with* SALOME.

Now to the wall to hear the Romans talk,
Observe their wiles, and study them to balk.

KALIPHILUS.

KALIPHILUS.

I AM entangled in the web I weave.
I shall but miss the mark which I would pierce
By bending that obdurate Simon. Help,
O Father of all Lies, help me invent.
Should I not lift some counterpoise, and check
The mounting zeal and palace-ward ambition
Of that dupe Simon, he will surely thwart
My purpose, moving forward to its goal
With steady pace; for he will slay Salome
To purchase, as he thinks, the Victory,
And so securely sit upon the throne.
Thus the one changeless aim of all my life
Shall shoot awry. But she must yet be mine
For love, or for revenge, as she shall choose.
Oh, she shall pay me for the woe she's caused.
Oh, she shall lighten, for one hour, my curse,
Since she alone hath placed it on my life.
But for this star, an aimless wanderer

Through Chaos tenfold raging should I drive,
A wreck that cannot sink — that cannot sink!
I will to John, and with some ready tale
Make him my dupe and ally. Oh, the fools!
The cursing spirit moves in me again,
And I must cry (*calling*), *Woe to the city!
woe!*

Enter SIMON.

SIMON.

Did'st hear that cry?

KALIPHILUS.

What cry?

SIMON.

Woe to the city!

KALIPHILUS.

Yea.

SIMON.

What bodes it?

KALIPHILUS.

Some wretch by hunger crazed
Sees in himself the city all accursed.

SIMON.

I came to seek thee, for the Romans now

Demand a parley, and I fain would know
What I shall answer.

KALIPHILUS.

Yield them not a whit,
Whate'er they ask. Defy them, and be firm.

ROMAN SOLDIERS, *at ease.*

CHORUS, *Roman Soldiers.*

Now rest.
In the west
Phœbus is sinking in blood.
Redder and redder he grows
As he goes
Plunging adown the red flood.
And Diana with fear
Starts from her couch, forgetting her veil,
And turns pale
To see her lord so disappear.
And the stars,
In glittering hosts following Mars,
Lift their spear points for lights
On Olympus' battlement heights,
And gaze down the Hesperian steeps
Where Phœbus still sinks in the deeps.
From the east swift rushes the Night,
Her visage all pale with affright;
And the winds,
Like fleet-footed hinds

Coursing over cerulean hills,
From their swift course refrain;
Upright is lifted each misty mane
At the premonition of ills
In the west.
Rest, comrades, rest.

Now rest
While a test,
To know if the gods be propitious,
Or if by beings malicious
Our fate is controlled,
The soothsayers hold.
And each to the gods an oblation
Shall pour,
That no more,
By this accursed nation,
Our arms shall suffer defeat.
No more we retreat.
For this night,
We swear by the light,
And the crest,
And the virgin breast
Of Diana, queen of the bow,
That we 'll hunt to their dens,
To their deadliest pens
Where their bloodiest treacheries grow,
To their eyries steep,

To their caverns deep,
This surly, serpent-like, swooping foe;
While every blow
Shall be a Roman's best.
Rest, comrades, rest.

Enter JOSEPHUS *and* ATTENDANTS.

JOSEPHUS.

Retire, my friends, retire, and give us place.

[*Exeunt* SOLDIERS.

O God of David, give my cause success.

Enter on the wall, SIMON *and* ATTENDANTS.

SIMON.

What would the Romans? Who shall speak
for Titus?

JOSEPHUS.

'T is I, Josephus.

SIMON.

Craven, art thou there?
'T is easy to foretell what shall be said
When traitors are the spokesmen.

JOSEPHUS.

I am here
To speak the words of Titus; not to rail,
Or answer railings. Hear ye: If so be
That ye are bent maliciously to fight,

Come out with John; heal your accursed sedi-
    tions,
And, with united forces, in the field
Engage the Romans. So shall ye preserve
The city and the Temple, nor offend,
More than ye have, the God of Abraham
By the defilement of His holy house.
And so the sacrifice, which now hath ceased,
Again may burn; for whomsoe'er ye choose
Shall worthy be esteemed to offer it.

SIMON.

Entice us not. Thy words are an offense.
For who can hear him speak that counts his life
In slavery to be preferred to death?
Deserter, traitor, coward, dost thou think
That we shall listen to thy craven counsel?
Or that we fear destruction of the city?
Or that the Almighty cannot guard His house?

JOSEPHUS.

Thine indignation at me is most just.
I merit treatment worse than thou canst tender,
Since here I strive to press deliverance
On those whom God already hath condemned.
Oh surely have ye kept the city pure!
Oh surely is the Temple undefiled!
Still offered is the daily sacrifice!

Oh, wretched cheat, dost thou then hope that
    God
Whom ye have robbed of His pure worship;
    whose
Pure Temple ye, with every crime, pollute;
Whose priests ye 've slain, e'en in the holy place,
Will aid you so to carry on the war,
In which such things are done, till ye shall
    triumph?
Behold! The city is hemmed in, and ye
Are prisoners. The wall, impassable,
Invests your hosts, and Cæsar is their keeper.
Within, his allies daily are at work
To mine your stubbornness, and bring you down.
For Famine hath a guard in every house
Sedition holds the streets, and Pestilence
Commands the gates; while Conflagration sits
Above the Temple with his flames in leash.
Antonia is Cæsar's. Banks are built
And rise like threatening waves; his engines,
    placed,
Are like the storm-clouds on a heaving sea.
The ready storm shall burst. Oh, yield in time.
E'en enemies and heathen now bemoan
The wretchedness that ye have brought upon
The city, and your sacrilegious crimes,
And for the shrine defiled their hot tears fall.
Oh, be persuaded, if ye will not do it,

And suffer Titus to preserve the city,
Our holy Temple, and religious rites.
Lo! Titus prays you to prevent the fire
Which hangs above the Temple to consume it.

SIMON.

Hast thou aught other message for mine ear?
If not, thy coming and thy words are useless.

JOSEPHUS.

Then on your own heads be the awful guilt.

SIMON.

Upon our heads and on our children's be it.

JOSEPHUS.

I have another message for thine ear.

SIMON.

Speak briefly, then.

JOSEPHUS.

   The Roman general Sextus,
Within the walls allured, was slain, or taken
A prisoner. The city, too, contains
Salome, daughter of Herodias,
With certain of her friends and dear attendants.
If Sextus live, I come to ransom him.

12

If he live not, I come to ask his body.
And, last, to ask that freely thou permit
Salome and her friends to leave the city.

SIMON.

Then hast thou come in vain.

JOSEPHUS.

Do not refuse
To reckon thine own gain conceding this.

SIMON.

My gains are reckoned, and I hold them fast.
Return to Titus, beg him to restrain
His swift impatience till the morning dawn.
Then shall he find displayed upon the wall
The bodies which he seeks.

JOSEPHUS.

And wilt thou dare
His vengeance by their murder?

SIMON.

Thou shalt see.
His vengeance is not terrible to me.
Give voice, ye trumpets, that no more we hear
The supplications of the coward Fear.

In the Temple.

KALIPHILUS *and* JOHN.

KALIPHILUS.

I TELL thee Simon shall thy master be —

JOHN.

The usurping robber! Make such prophecies
To those who 'll hear them. Never, while I
    live,
Can this be true, false prophet, his accomplice —

KALIPHILUS.

I tell thee Simon shall thy master be,
And king of all the Jews, unless I aid thee.

JOHN.

Thou com'st to tell me this? A useless mis-
    sion.
How much hath Simon paid thee for this song?
What! thinkest thou that it shall make me shake,
Undo my courage, put my hopes to flight,
And overthrow the walls of my resolve?

Or hopest thou to drain my treasury?
For how much would'st thou sell thy proffered
    aid?

KALIPHILUS.

Believe or disbelieve as facts shall prove.
My aid I proffer freely; I but ask
That thou accept it and be ruled by me.
For I can point the way, which, if thou follow,
'T is thou shalt mount above him and prevail.

JOHN.

Well, map it out; and when it shall be seen,
I 'll tell thee whether thou shalt be my captain.

KALIPHILUS.

Know, then, that Simon holds a Roman captive.
A princess, who to-morrow shall be led
As 't were to execution on the wall:
Thus shall the vengeful multitude consent
To let her pass. But, once upon the wall,
'T is Simon's purpose to deliver her
To Titus, and her ransom to be paid,
As is already secretly agreed,
Shall be the sovereignty of this shamed people,
Under the Romans. Simon's forces then,
With Cæsar's host united, shall compel
Obedience —

JOHN.

The traitorous villain!

KALIPHILUS.

Now,
If thou would'st snatch this vantage from his
grasp,
Prepare a rescue secretly —

JOHN.

And then —

KALIPHILUS.

Let chosen men be ready ere the dawn,
And thou shalt lead them; thee will I direct.
And, that thou fail not, see thy force be strong.
They other prisoners have, for whom their care
Shall be thy ally; for the General Sextus,
As thou hast heard, shall then be crucified.

JOHN.

And if I rescue her?

KALIPHILUS.

Then bring her straight
Into the Temple, place her in my guard,
And I will answer that she leave me not.
To Titus then, as thine ambassador,
Will I repair, obtain such terms for thee
As he hath pledged to Simon —

JOHN.

It is well,
And fairly hast thou spoken. 'T is agreed.
The men shall ready be, and of the best.
Where is this prisoner?

KALIPHILUS.

In the castle dungeon.

JOHN.

Let me but know the hour when she shall
        leave it,
And I will fail thee not. How is she called?

KALIPHILUS.

Salome, daughter of Herodias.

A Dungeon.

SALOME.

SALOME.

In this dread dungeon, where I heard with joy
  The holy teachings and the gentle voice
Of John the Baptist, let me now employ
  Remaining strength to wonder and rejoice,
For mercy infinite, which doth not scorn
To stay and save me, wandering and forlorn.

Whatever trials Thou shalt think it meet
  To send me, Saviour, let me not repine;
But count myself most blessèd, at Thy feet
  To suffer for the joy of being Thine, —
Adoring still the Pity and the Love
Which stoops to raise me to Thy home above.

My Father, in this scene of my great crime,
  Oh make me as a little child again.
Make me forget the weary, sinful time,
  That I have passed in penitence and pain.
As from his lips I heard his pardoning word,
So now by me Thy pardoning voice be heard.

And as he died, let me prepare to die,
  Forgiving all, and trusting in Thy grace,
That Thou wilt call me to Thyself on high,
  And that I there again shall see his face,
Assured of pardon, saved, and sanctified,
Though worst of all for whom the Saviour died.

Enter THONA *and* CHORUS *of Christians.*

O friends, why come ye to the lion's lair?

CHORUS.

We come to share what may betide thee there.

SALOME.

But wot ye not our enemies prevail?

CHORUS.

Should we in such an hour of trial fail?

SALOME.

It was a comfort to believe you fled.

CHORUS.

Fly thou, and let us suffer in thy stead.

THONA.

I could not leave thee. I would die with thee.

SALOME.

Nay, it is fit I die, but ye should flee.

CHORUS.

For if the Bridegroom with His train this night
Appear, shall we be scattered hence in flight?
Shall we not, with our lamps well trimmed, go
    meet Him?
With wedding garments on, go forth to greet
    Him?
Arise, stand ready. If to-night our guide
Be taken from us, where shall we abide?

Enter SEXTUS.

SEXTUS.

Ah! I have come in time. The Lord be praised.
And they would torture thee —

SALOME.

Oh! Art thou crazed —

SEXTUS.

Dear hands, untouched; those feet, this gentle
    form —

SALOME.

That thou defiest thus this fatal storm?

SEXTUS.

They would torment thee — yet thou art unharmed?

SALOME.

For thee, alone, my heart is now alarmed.

SEXTUS.

They 'd make thee me betray with tortured
breath.

SALOME.

And thou for this hast come to certain death?

SEXTUS.

Most gladly, if to save thee but one sigh.

SALOME.

My sighs so saved, who should sigh more than I?

SEXTUS.

What pangs had I if I from thee had fled.

SALOME.

And I, what sorrows thus to know thee dead.

SEXTUS.

Who takes me hence, shall hew me from thee,
love.

SALOME.

Together to His rest we shall remove.

CHORUS.

Now, led by Love, let golden-winged Content
From its calm realm descend, and in its hands
Take these true hearts, by weary trials spent,
Through crystal portals lead them to blest lands,
Whose firm foundations no commotions jar,
Whose perfect joy no gloomy fate can mar.

A Room in the Castle.

MARAH.

Nay, but it may be done. Some one inspired
By love of country, pity for our people,
Could find the way to Cæsar's tent, and there
Send his too mounting spirit down to Hades.
The will and purpose, which now guides the
    siege,
Should faint and die; and all his army then,
Confused and terrified, should fall a prey
To well directed sallies from the wall.

SIMON.

Zeal, courage, vengeance, all inspire our men,
Whose deeds of daring make all others cowards.
And they as gladly would the venture make
As, starving now, they'd rush unto a feast;
Think him most happy whom I should permit
To undertake the deed. But it were vain.
No man could cross the boundaries of their
    camp.

MARAH.

What man cannot perchance a woman can.
As our own Judith ventured to the lair
Of Holofernes, and with his own brand
Slew him, and overthrew his conquering host;
So some fair woman, daughter of her soul,
Might Cæsar slay and save this sinking nation.

SIMON.

But, in these days, who is there, brave and fair,
The peril of such enterprise to dare?

MARAH.

I would not boast, yet fain would I essay —

SIMON.

Thou, foolish woman! but to rue the day.

MARAH.

Nay, Simon, I can do it; thine shall be
The glory of the deed; enough for me
To seem but in thy hands the instrument
For this great action. Give me thy consent,
And I will pledge success. Oh, let me go
And save this people from this sea of woe.

SIMON.

How could'st thou, feeble, reach his guarded tent?
How do the deed on which thy soul is bent?

MARAH.

Let forty chosen men of courage tried,
In whom discretion is with wit allied,
Attired as women in dark garbs of woe,
With forms low bent and long veils falling
    low,
Go with me as the ministers of fate,
That I may seem attended by a state.
Then, as a princess, come to intercede
For justice, or for clemency to plead,
To offer peace, or ask peace-making truce,
Some favor beg, or argue some abuse,
Shall I be brought before him.   There I'll
    find
The occasion and the way to do my mind.

SIMON.

Such men I have ; such garments they might
    wear.
But would'st thou, truly, so much peril dare ?

MARAH.

Oh! would I dare it, Simon?   For me, death
Is dearer now than is my hated breath.
And I was fair — Oh would I had not been ! —
Perchance by hope and noble thoughts within
This beauty may relighted be, and then,
As me it periled, shall it peril men.

SIMON.

If Titus brave and generous shall prove
The fool that Fame reports him, grief shall
    move
His soul e'en more than beauty. In thine eye
A thousand dangerous provocations lie,
Which, seemingly disarmed by grief and pain,
Shall, unsuspected, their advantage gain.

MARAH.

If in the venture I shall nobly fall,
My noble death shall blot my failings all.

SIMON.

And, if success shall crown thee, then loud fame
Shall drown the whisperings of envious blame.
I know thou hast a firm and daring soul,
To mount for victory and reach the goal.
So go, and prosper. Here thou shalt await,
And presently I 'll hither bring thy state,
The men accoutred, ready to thy mind,
To help thee strongly bound as oaths can bind.
                    [*Exit* SIMON.

MARAH.

A traitress, too! What then ? No crime can
    now
Add to my infamy, or plunge me deeper
In dark Gehenna. O Jerusalem,

I do it for thy sake, beloved city, —
And hers, — lest others weakly do as I,
Like me constrained, and make thee a reproach,
Themselves accursed.   Is treason then a crime,
If I betray thee for thy good and theirs?
Deceit, when merciful, no more deceit
But mercy is, for holy beings meet.
Yet they shall call me traitress, say I sold
My faith, my nation, for more life, for gold,
For luxury — oh! luxury for me
To die, and what now haunts me no more see;
To know the strength so ill obtained hath
        served
To bless some hearts from ills like mine pre-
        served.
Is there no pity in the heavens for strength
O'erborne? for souls in utter misery foundered?
If I may take a life to save mine own
When threatened by that life, why may I not
Howe'er my life be threatened? life is life.
And my child's life, already half mine own,
In taking it I took but half a life,
And sent him innocent from woes impending.

Enter SIMON, *and* SOLDIERS *disguised as women.*

SIMON.

Behold the men.

MARAH.

Are they instructed all?
Can they be trusted, whatsoe'er befall?

SIMON.

Ay, faithful, ready, of discretion best,
They will obey, unquestioned, thy behest.

MARAH.

Then count my purpose acted ere the day
Light up the shores of morning with its ray.

SIMON.

The elements of nature threaten war,
And rising winds, night's sighs, are heard from
    far.
Black jagged clouds, like huge Tartarean bulls,
With heads low bent, rush roaring to the fray,
And breathe from hissing nostrils lurid flames.

MARAH.

Let them o'erthrow the heavens, my purpose
    holds.

SIMON.

I hear, as 't were, the echoes of wild laughter,
And gibbering voices mock the startled ear
From out the darkness; whispers from the clouds

13

Like falling snow flakes melt or ere the sense
Can grasp their chilly meaning —

MARAH.

Dost thou fear?
Well may thy trembling conscience make thee
    shake.
And ye, my friends, shall terrors make ye fail,
Or will ye with me o'er them all prevail?

CHORUS, *Soldiers.*

So dark as is the deed should be
The darkness it concealing.   See!
The eyes of heaven are shut.   Away!
Let it be finished ere the day.

Cæsar's Pavilion.

TITUS, LEPIDUS, FRIGIUS, *and the* COMMANDERS OF LEGIONS.

TITUS.

COMPANIONS, and dear sharers of our toils,
Now Victory smiles upon our enterprise.
The omens are propitious, and the gods
Descend in mighty shadows from the hills,
As in the time while Troy yet was; their tread
The heavens shakes; their clashing armor sounds
Reverberating thunders through the air,
And gleams in livid lightnings from the clouds,
Which veil their awful majesties from view.
They move in dreadful presence to the fight.
On with them; let our deeds illume this night.
Brave Lepidus shall, with a chosen band,
Stand ready till the breachèd wall invite;
Then his shall be the honor to invade
The portal opened by your enginery,
And cut his way into the castle, there
To plant our standard on the topmost tower,
And free our Sextus who lies there enchained,
And others dear to Rome and dear to him, —

While each of you your several powers shall
     press
Through breaches, broken gates, and falling
     towers,
To seize their strongholds and to storm the
     Temple.
But this I charge you, let no daring hand
Put to that house the sacrilegious brand.
Such is our plan, which, Valor seconding,
Shall lead us to the end of these our labors,
Entice wreath-bearing Victory, and Fame,
Her swift-winged herald, to our conquering
     camp,
And bring the Muses down to celebrate
Our triumphs and the victor's sweet rewards.
Go, Lepidus, with blessings of the gods.
Thy mission is most dangerous; its cause
Most just and holy; so the undertaking
Most honorable. Perils, undisguised
And hidden, wait for thee; perchance defeat
In ambush lies as the van-guard of death.
Dishonor, Lepidus, cannot o'ertake thee,
Nor lies it in thy path. And, if thou win,
I'd give my hopes of empire for thy glory,
And think I'd paid thee naught, so great thy
     gain.
I envy thee, my friend. Oh would the gods
Had made my duty lie where goes my wish,

And Titus thy lieutenant then had been,
And death in this adventure better loved
Than life remaining here. O Lepidus,
I know thy heart is made of heroism,
By Disappointment tempered, and thy zeal
Is forged and hardened by Adversity —
A very Vulcan when he worketh on
True metal — to the bow of steel, resolve,
Which will not be unbent till the arrow, purpose,
Shall pierce the centre of the targe, success.
Yet let my exhortation add some strength
To the right arm of thy determination,
That I may seem not idle in the achievement,
And share some part of favor in the end
Of thy great work. The gods be with thee,
         friend.

LEPIDUS.

Thy friend shall still deserve thy friendship,
         Titus,
In life or death. So, for the night, farewell.

TITUS.

To thee, O Frigius, I will but say
That Lepidus hath chosen well. Approve
His choice of a lieutenant. Fare ye well.

               [*Exeunt* LEPIDUS *and* FRIGIUS.

You, generals, each to his station move,
And when ye see Destruction's fiery banner

Flung from Antonia's tower to the skies,
Its flaming folds red gleaming from the smoke
Tartareous that hangeth ever round it,
And drapeth it in awe-inspiring black,
Let every engine answer with its bolts
To heaven's dread enginery, and the loud crash
Of swift artillery outdo the thunder,
And, while your rushing legions shake the earth,
O'erthrow the walls and towers; then to the
    breaches.
Great Caesar's constellation in the heavens
With anxious eagerness regardeth trembling,
And starteth forward from its azure seat,
To see Rome's soldiers fight as did his Romans;
And their commander watcheth to reward.
Rome, rising from her seven hills, looketh on.
Go, with the favor of the most just gods.

                    [*Exeunt* COMMANDERS.

O god of battles, Mars omnipotent,
If I have been a worthy son; if e'er
My fathers served thee; if thou hast respect
To Rome; if she, thy priestess, crimson in
Thy robes, hath been accepted; for her sake,
And for my fathers', and thine honor, Mars,
Hear now my prayer. Oh give mine arms
    success;
But spare the Temple. Let the city's wreck
Suffice; and let this glory of the earth

Remain. Bid flames down to their kennels.
    Turn
The lightnings back. Or if, for jealousy,
Thou would'st destroy this Temple to a god
Who on Olympus hath no place, forbear,
And I will build to thee a shrine so great
That jealousy nor envy can o'erlook
Its lofty walls and towers and battlements.

Enter an OFFICER.

OFFICER.

A Hebrew woman with a courtly train
Awaits, and craves admission to thy presence.

TITUS.

How did she pass the barriers of the camp?

OFFICER.

They were arrested, and she prayed at once
To be conducted hither, arguing
Some business of great import.

TITUS.

           Bid her come
Alone, and let her train attend without.
              [*Exit* OFFICER.

Some wretched creature fled from wretchedness

In the doomed city. They will have it so.
I would have spared them; but the gods are
   just.

Enter OFFICER *with* MARAH.

Approach and do thine errand. She is faint:
Give her some wine.

MARAH.

     Thanks, gracious Cæsar, thanks.
Thy clemency and goodness are well known.
But I came not to plead for clemency.
In briefest phrase I will my speech unfold :
Salome, daughter of Herodias,
A prisoner in the castle, held by Simon,
Is doomed, to-morrow, to be crucified.
The general Sextus, living and in health,
A prisoner in the castle, held by Simon,
Is doomed, to-morrow, to be crucified.
The miserable remnant of my people,
Imprisoned in the city by thine arms,
Is daily crucified by every ill
That utter wretchedness can summon. Now
They helpless lie, the very sport of Death.
The daily sacrifice hath failed for need
Of men to offer it. And now we know
The end. The oracle, long writ, declares
That, when the oblation and the sacrifice
Shall cease, in dreadful floods of desolation

The predetermined consummation comes.
And silence which shall mock the ear will tell
Where stood Mount Zion, glory of the earth.
The Lord of all the earth He shall do right.
His will be done. And, since it is His will
That thou should'st take the city and prevail,
I come to proffer my weak aid, and save,
If it may be, some poor souls from perdition,
Who, having suffered with meek resignation,
Yet, overtempted by their misery,
May do some dreadful deed against our laws
And fall to reprobation ; as some have.

TITUS.

Give her somewhat to eat.

MARAH.

I will not eat
Till I shall have accomplished all my vow.

TITUS.

How canst thou aid us ? What can we for thee ?

MARAH.

Prepare me forty men, your best and bravest ;
But, first, secure my train which waits without,
And guard them hostages for these ye send.
They all are men in women's vestments hid ;

For Simon, thinking that I hither came
To take thy life, hath greatly favored me,
And I shall have free ingress to the city,
And to the castle, with my company.

TITUS.

Go on, go on.

MARAH.

And let thy forty men
With these disguises, which mine own have
worn,
Induc themselves —

TITUS.

Now I perceive thy scheme :
Go, summon Lepidus.

[*Exit* OFFICER.

MARAH.

And they, by me
Led to the castle, while your fierce assault
Shall call its garrison to man the walls,
Shall easily possess it, and set free
Both Sextus and Salome. Terror then
Shall fall on the seditious in the city,
When they shall see thy standards on its towers,
And know the castle held by thee, — themselves
Between the upper and the nether millstone.
And so thou shalt prevail.

TITUS.

I would not doubt
Such seeming faith, but caution aye becomes
The soldier.   Hast thou then no token brought ?

MARAH.

I have.   Behold the signet-ring of Sextus.

TITUS.

Enough, and for this service thou shalt learn
How Rome and Cæsar can be grateful.   Now
Thou shalt be general of this expedition,
And every thing be ordered by thy wish.

Court of the Castle.

SIMON.

THE Future stands, with open arms, before me,
And, smiling, whispers promises most fair,
Now half fulfilled. Thou art my prophet prince ;
For, since Salome hath been in my power,
And sentenced, all things are propitious to me.

KALIPHILUS.

Thy faith shall win for thee the warrior's
    crown —
But swerve not from the course I have pre-
    scribed.

SIMON.

By this time Marah hath, in Cæsar's camp,
Subdued his heart and taken his proud head.
She knoweth skillfully how to evoke,
From their dark covert in the heart profound,
The treacherous passions, keep them well in
    check,
Their mistress ever, that they rend her not.
As traitors, gained in citadels besieged,

They put the eyes of sovereign Judgment out,
Enchain the ready garrison of Thoughts,
And drive beneath the yoke the captive Will
With scourges. So, all unsuspected, she
Ere this hath taken Titus, and I wait
Impatiently her coming.

KALIPHILUS.

Trust her not;
For she would rather make one man her slave
Than free a nation. She is but a woman.
And, if perchance his manly parts invite
Her to the attack, while Prudence her defies,
And calm Indifference seem invulnerable,
In the hot vigor of her first assault
She shall forget to guard the avenues
And gates which open to her inmost heart.
And so he shall but wait his vantage time
To take possession of, and be her master.
Nay, rather disregard this foolish scheme,
And, as I bid thee, climb to victory.

SIMON.

And when I shall be victor, thou shalt be
My chiefest counselor, and, if thou wilt,
High priest. Nay, choose thyself thy guerdon, so
It take thee not from me. I would not lose
Thy counsel and direction.

KALIPHILUS.

Fear me not,
For sooner thou shalt drive me hence than I
Thy fortunes cease to govern.

SIMON.

Ho ! already
I seem to feel the crown upon my brow,
And breathe the regal air.

KALIPHILUS.

But tell me now,
What order hast thou taken to fulfill
My mandate ? She shall die how, when, and
    where ?

SIMON.

When first the gleaming harbingers of morn
In golden armor mount the eastern clouds,
Shall she be taken to the valley gate.
And when the sun, for his unrivaled course,
Shall stand prepared upon the eastern hills,
She shall be crucified upon the wall,
And, with her, Sextus. Dost thou this approve ?

KALIPHILUS.

Ay, it is well. See that thou change it not.

SIMON.

And shall I then be crowned? Will all the factions
Unite and hail me master of the city?
And Victory lead our conjoinèd hosts
To overthrow the Romans, drive them hence,
And bar them from the realm of Palestine?

KALIPHILUS.

A sound, in heaven, of rolling chariot wheels!
And cries of squadrons rushing into battle!

SIMON.

Ah! whence this sudden night-devouring light?

KALIPHILUS.

The tower Antonia is on fire! and up
To heaven extendeth supplicating arms
Of flame! O elements, what shall be now?

Enter an OFFICER.

OFFICER.

Ho! they assault. The Romans beat the walls,
And knock so at the gates that they will open
Of their accord without the aid of porters—

SIMON.

Then cry, To arms! Ho! All men to the walls!

Call out the garrison, and let the wardens
Care for the castle! Simon to the rescue!

[*Exeunt* SIMON *and* OFFICER.

KALIPHILUS.

So, all goes well, and at the appointed hour
Shall John be ready with his chosen power
To rescue her. Let Sextus' soul descend,
Then is she mine until her brief life end.
And then — then — but anticipation dread,
And woful retrospection! Drear and dead
The world's great wilderness; no hope to see
Aught sympathizing, feared or loved by me.
Once more within my power, O ready skill,
Invent the way for mine opposeless will,
So that, escaped from factions and alarms,
No force but Death shall tear her from mine
        arms.
But can I safely trust this night's wild chances?
These dire portents most wonderful declare
Some most unheard disaster. Shall I wait
The coming of the morn, whose tearful eye
May blinded be by smoke of conflagrations,
The only dwellers then in this cursed city?
Or, boldly, on my single arm rely,
And my well practiced wit to take her hence?
Now all is dark. No wreck of light illumes
The deep of tossing clouds. The stars are sunk,

All foundered, all their glittering spars gone
    down.
And in the darkness and chaotic rush,
Perchance unchallenged, I could pass with her,
The dearest thing to me in that dear world,
The last thing left to me from that lost world,
That Paradise I dwelt in ere my curse.

Enter an OFFICER.

Whence comest thou ? What news ? How goes
    the fight ?
OFFICER.

I come from Simon, ordered to behead
Salome in the dungeon.

KALIPHILUS.

Wherefore thus ?

OFFICER.

The Romans press our powers on every side ;
And Simon will cast forth the accursed thing
To turn the anger of the Lord of Hosts.

KALIPHILUS.

And I command thee to remain with me,
Until the accepted hour arrive. Stay! halt!
Or I will curse thee. Simon doth not well.
To yonder gallery ascend, report

14

From time to time the movements of the fight.
I will the moment indicate when thou
Shalt strike the blow and win the victory.

[OFFICER *ascends.*

I must gain time, or all is lost — gain time!
I feel my power slip from me. Help, ye fiends!
The vision of my soul is dimmed; in vain
I seek some subtle stratagem. O devils!

CHORUS *without, Priests.*

Eloi, Eloi, lama sabachthani?

OFFICER, *above.*

Like the impenetrable adamant
Which, blackened, stands the topless bourne of
    hell,
The clouds down to the earth are packed in
    walls
Of smooth and pitchy darkness, which surround
The Temple, city, and the flaming pile.
While, overhead, in the fierce flame's hot glare,
They redly roll, and turn, and sink, and surge,
Like bloody seas vexed by a tempest, or
Some crimson lake of fire — hell in the heavens.
The ebon walls divide, and lightning streams
Flash through like wrath which burneth hot
    beyond.

CHORUS *without;* PRIESTS *passing.*

Eloi, Eloi, lama sabachthani ?

KALIPHILUS.

Forsaken ! Ay, forsaken ! Roar, ye priests.

OFFICER, *above.*

Light with a million arrowy rays again .
Hath pierced the breast of brooding darkness.
    Ah !
The Temple is on fire ! The eastern gate
Glares like the shield of Morning when he
    drives
Night's rout of shadows to their northern caves.

CHORUS *without;* PRIESTS *receding.*

Eloi, Eloi, lama sabachthani ?

Enter MARAH, LEPIDUS, FRIGIUS, *and* SOLDIERS *disguised as women.*

MARAH.

Secure the gate, and make the castle yours.

LEPIDUS.

Away these trappings, as yourselves appear.
Good Frigius, up to the battlements :
Unveil the Roman standard.

                                    [*Exit* FRIGIUS.

Some of you
Secure these men, and guard them while we
search
The castle.

[KALIPHILUS *and* OFFICER *are bound.*

The garrison made prisoners,
We'll to the dungeon. Here wait my return.

[*Exit* LEPIDUS *with Attendants.*

CHORUS *without;* JEWS, *going away captive.*

Fare ye well! farewell, O palaces deserted!
Fare thee well! farewell, O city desolated!
Fare thee well! farewell, O glory now de-
parted!
Fare thee well! farewell, O Temple desecrated!
How are the mighty brought low! Kings in
the harness have fallen.
Queens are a prey to the spoiler; princes are
bent under burdens.
Gone from their dwellings the people, — gone,
or silent forever.
Mourning is heard there no more; there are
the dead and the voiceless.
Silent the sheep in the sheep-cote; there the
wolf howleth and raveneth:
There were no shepherds to watch, no hedge
to protect and defend them.

God, our Shepherd, hath left us ; God hath condemned and forsaken.

God hath opened the vials; wrath raineth fiercely upon us.

Save, O save us, Death: the heathen are our masters!

Save, O save us, Death, from those who lead us captive!

Save, O save us, Death, from insult and reviling!

Save, O save us, Death, from life a burden to us!

A Dungeon.

Sextus, Salome, Thona, *and* Chorus *of Christians.*

CHORUS.

Though I walk through
The valley of the shadow
Of death,
Yet will I fear no evil,
For Thou art with me.

SALOME.

He will be with us, if we trust in Him,
And He shall soon receive us to Himself.

CHORUS.

In my Father's house are many mansions :
If it were not so, I would have told you.
I go to prepare a place for you,
That where I am, there ye may be also.

SEXTUS.

The tumult waxes, and the Roman shout
Can now be heard. Our friends will take us
hence.

E'en now they come ! and we are saved. Shall have
Yet many days to love and help each other.

Enter MARAH, LEPIDUS, FRIGIUS, TORCH BEARERS, *and* SOLDIERS *with* KALIPHILUS, *bound.*

LEPIDUS.

My Thona ! Where 's my Thona ?

THONA.

Here. Oh here.

SEXTUS.

Dear Lepidus, brave Frigius, ye 've done
A deed such as ye only know to do —

LEPIDUS.

Nay, it was Marah, here, who hath performed
Such acts as have our Roman women crowned.

SALOME.

God bless thee, Marah, as our hearts now bless.

SEXTUS.

We 'll give thee better thanks ere long, but now —

MARAH.

I pray ye, let my actions pass in silence.

SEXTUS.

But is the city taken?

LEPIDUS.

It shall be,
If not already —

SEXTUS.

Thou art safe, Salome.
To-morrow we together will set out
For Rome. There shall we be so happy. Then
Shall joy make swift amends for our past grief.
There on the banks of Tiber, in my palace —

SALOME.

Nay, Sextus, I am bound unto a country
Above the earth, where there can be no grief.
There on the flowery banks of life's sweet river
Shall we in God's own palace dwell, — *An house
Not made with hands, eternal in the heavens.*

KALIPHILUS.

Salome, it was here John Baptist died.
Here I beheaded him — at thy request,
To please thee, dear one, but to win thy love —

SALOME.

Oh, help me.

SEXTUS.

Stop his mouth.

KALIPHILUS.

I took' his head
To give thee — 't was thy wish—for thee I
    did it —
He knew it too.   O innocent ! — O angel !—

LEPIDUS.

Lo ! Cæsar comes !

Enter TITUS, JOSEPHUS, *and* ATTENDANTS, *with* SIMON *a prisoner.*

Hail ! Imperator, hail !

TITUS.

The city 's ours, John ta'en, and Simon here
Our prisoner.

KALIPHILUS.

Ha, ha !   He would be king.

TITUS.

Good Lepidus, stout Frigius, true friends,
Ye need not Cæsar's praises.   Your reward
Ye here have won, and proudly shall ye boast it.

SALOME.

Hag, witch, thou didst betray me; thou she-
wolf—

[*Attempts to smite* MARAH.

TITUS.

Chain, take him hence. Preserve him for the
triumph.
He would be king. When, at the Capitol,
According to the rules of Roman triumphs,
He shall be slain, prepare a red-hot crown
And place it on his brows. He shall be crowned.

KALIPHILUS.

Ha, Simon! thou shalt yet be king. Hey, Si-
mon?
Dost feel the crown upon thy kingly brows,
And snuff the regal air? Hail! Simon, hail!

SIMON.

False prophet, liar, O fiend, accursed—

KALIPHILUS.

Ha, ha!
[SIMON *is led out.*

TITUS.

Brave Marah, it shall be my charge to see
That thou hast a reward commensurate
With thy great merit. Cæsar's gratitude

Thou hast already, and the Emperor
Shall learn thy noble deeds. Rome loves brave
    women.
Salome, Cæsar hails and welcomes thee,
The Emperor's guest, with these thy faithful
    friends ;
And, midst rejoicings for this victory,
Shall Sextus claim thee as his loving wife.
Then Lepidus shall take his dear love home,
Whom I salute. Thou art worthy of him,
    Thona,
And that is praise such as few women win.
Now let us leave this dungeon. For your
    need
Already food and wine have been prepared.

KALIPHILUS (*having silently freed himself from his bonds*).

Sir, by thy leave —

[*Snatches a sword and thrusts at* SEXTUS; SALOME *springs
before him and receives the blow.*

SALOME.

Oh! I am slain! Ah! Sextus —

[*Swoons.*

SEXTUS.

Salome! Speak! What! dead! by that fell
    hand!
Nay, friends, stand back — give me a sword —
    stand back,

And let me deal with him. We have a question
Must be discussed with bloody arguments.

[*Attacks* KALIPHILUS.

KALIPHILUS.

Now she is dead, live on, and be accursed
Like me. Live on. Hold, play not with me, or
I shall be kinder to thee than I would.
What! wilt thou then? Ha! wilt thou? Have
    it so.

[*Stabs* SEXTUS.

SEXTUS.

I could not stay. I come to thee, Salome.

[*Dies.*

TITUS.

Straight scourge him hence, ay, scourge him
    till he die.
And weary not in scourging —

KALIPHILUS.

                  Ha, ha! come,
And one by one I'll rid me of your stings.

[*Exit* KALIPHILUS, *pursued by* SOLDIERS *scourging him.*

SALOME.

Come rear me, Sextus — Thona — ah! — Fare-
    well.
Come, Sextus, — come — come. Lord, receive
    my spirit.

[*Dies.*

CHORUS, *Romans.*

So upon the dim shore breaks the mist en-
shrouded billow.

CHORUS, *Christians.*

So the stars are lost in light when the full
day appeareth.

CHORUS, *Romans.*

Now to the Islands of the Blessed oh waft
them, waft them,
Ye gentle gales, that, o'er the mystic seas soft
moving,
Convey each soul freighted with honesty and
virtue
To that dear haven. And there in sunny
bays, by shore lands,
Wood-covered, flower-embroidered, filled with
sweets and music,
Let these storm-beaten souls at anchor rest
forever.

CHORUS, *Christians.*

Bléssèd are the dead who die in Jesus,
For they rest, they rest from all their labors.
Now they wing their way unto the city
Where the Prince of Peace forever reigneth.
Dark are the portals of death ; beyond them is
brightness eternal.

They who have passed them are washed and
clothed in glories unfading.
Death is the messenger sent to make of the
mortal the immortal, —
To lead from without the lost children within
to the halls of their Father.

A VOICE *above*.

What are these arrayed in shining raiment?

CHORUS *above, many voices*.

These are they which came from mighty tribu-
lation,
And have washed their robes and made them
white and spotless
In the blood of Christ, the slain Lamb, their
Redeemer.
No more shall they hunger, never more be thirsty;
Nor the sun shall fall, nor any heat, upon them:
From their eyes, by Him, shall every tear be
wipèd.

THE END.

www.ingramcontent.com/pod-product-compliance
Lightning Source LLC
Chambersburg PA
CBHW030130030726
47498CB00007B/2636